Box

of

Treasures

N. CAVELL

ELECTIO PUBLISHING
first century principles.
a twenty-first century approach.

Box of Treasures

By N. Cavell

Copyright 2018 by N. Cavell. All rights reserved.

Cover Design by eLectio Publishing.

ISBN-13: 978-1-63213-496-7

Published by eLectio Publishing, LLC

Little Elm, Texas

http://www.eLectioPublishing.com

5 4 3 2 1 eLP 22 21 20 19 18

The eLectio Publishing creative team is comprised of: Kaitlyn Hallmark, Emily Certain, Lori Draft, Court Dudek, Jim Eccles, Sheldon James, and Christine LePorte.

Publisher's Note

ACKNOWLEDGMENTS

First and foremost, I want to thank you, daddy God. For it was you who placed this story on my heart and then encouraged me to share it with others. Thank you for walking with me through this journey called life, through the ups and downs. For never leaving me nor forsaking me, (Deuteronomy 31:6). Even during those times where you felt so distant, you were right beside me. For the forgiveness of my sins through your son Jesus, (Romans 3:23-26). No sin is too big for you to forgive; you have removed all my sin, past, present and future as far as the east is from the west (Psalm 103:12). For making me a new creation, (2 Corinthians 5:17). For your love, (John 3:16). And for the hope those of us who believe in your son Jesus have, looking forward to an eternity in your presence (Revelation 21 & 22 1:5). Second, I want to thank my husband. Without your help and support, without you feeding, schooling, bathing, and occupying our children, I would never have found the time to sit down and write. And, last but not least, I thank eLectio Publishing, who took a chance on an unknown writer and made my dream of becoming a published author a reality.

PROLOGUE

July 2016

Standing in front of my kitchen sink, I looked out the window, watching several children as they played under the two large oaks. At one time, there had been three oaks, but almost twenty years ago now, one had been hit by lightning. Slowly the tree had died off, and a few years later, my son Andrew came over with his two sons and cut it down. My husband Miles was in his early eighties at the time, too old for hard labor anymore, though I remembered the days when he worked from dawn to dusk, mostly outdoors. By mid-spring, Miles had a tan that he kept through September. And his muscles . . . he was always so strong. How I would love to feel his arms around me once again. Of course, he had not been as strong as he once was for many years now, but I always felt safe, complete in his arms. Reaching up, I wiped my tears away, tears that came often these last few days. I tried to count the exact number of children, but it was near impossible as they were not still. I guessed there to be about thirty, most of which were my great-grandchildren, though a handful of the children belonged to other families who lived in the area. Miles was well known in the community and well-loved, and my house was full of people at the moment. At least three hundred people had come by to give their condolences. I smiled as I watched Ben, my eleven-year-old great-grandson, push his younger sister Annabelle on the swing. Annabelle clung tightly to the swing as Ben pushed, though she had a huge smile on her face. The sound of her sweet laughter carried in through the open window. *Oh, to be young again,* I thought to myself. *Young and carefree.* This old body of mine was full of aches and pains. I looked down at my hands. They were worn, thin, and wrinkled, just like the rest of me. I was once a beauty with chestnut brown hair, bright blue eyes, and a stunning figure, but that was many years ago now. "You alright, Mama?" I turned my head and smiled as my eldest daughter Nancy entered the kitchen. At sixty-nine and a grandmother herself, she too was no longer young, but she was still just as beautiful as she was the day she was born. It was hard to believe my children were all as old as they were. My eldest son Ethan was sixty-four. Both he and Nancy had birthdays coming up in September on which they would be yet another year older. Growing up, they always had combined birthday parties as their birthdays were only two days apart. Then came Andrew, who was sixty-two, and Jenny was sixty . . . or was she fifty-nine? I couldn't remember . . . another side effect of age. And Charlie, he was the baby at fifty-eight. It seemed like just yesterday they were all babies. Now my babies had babies, and many of their babies had babies. Where had the time gone? When I was young, life seemed like it would go on forever and forever, but now how relevant 1 Peter 1:24 seems. "All flesh is like grass and all its glory like the flower of grass. The grass withers, and the flower falls . . ." (ESV)

"You holding up alright, Mama?" Nancy asked as she placed her arm around me.

"Yes," I replied as I looked back out the window. "I'm just watching the children play."

The two of us stood side by side for several minutes, silently watching the children. Through the sounds of the children, I could hear a dog barking in the distance. Probably from one of the newer neighborhoods that were popping up all over the place. This farm was one of the last standing farms in the area. Over the years, the others had sold their lands off. Now shopping centers and neighborhoods surrounded our land. We too had sold a good amount of our land, though we sold it to our daughter Jenny and her husband who had kept it as a working farm. "I remember the day Daddy hung that swing," Nancy whispered, breaking our silence.

"Do you?" I asked, looking in her direction. Nancy nodded her response. "I'm surprised you remember. If I recall correctly, you were no more than five or six."

"Six. I was six, Mama," she said, smiling. "I had just started first grade, and Ethan was there too . . . he had just begun to walk. I remember you had to pick him up and hold him so I could try out the swing." I too smiled, remembering how excited Nancy was to have that swing, though I do believe Miles was just as excited to hang it as she was to have it. "I miss him, Mama," she said, her eyes filling with tears. "I miss Daddy."

Now it was I who put my arm around her. "I know you do, baby. I miss him too, but we'll see him again. We both know he's with Jesus. That he's not really gone, just in a different place . . . he is home."

Nancy nodded slightly, smiling—well, trying to force a smile though I could tell she just could not manage one. Hearing footsteps, I turned my head just as Ethan entered into the kitchen. "Mother, the guests are starting to leave," he said.

I nodded then took Nancy's hand in mine. "Come, let's go say goodbye."

***

I stood in the entry hall, looking around the old farmhouse. Other than my children, their spouses, and my granddaughter Eva, everyone else had left, and the house was now relatively quiet. Nancy, Jenny, Eva, and my three daughters-in-law were all making trips back and forth from the formal dining room into the kitchen, putting away all the food people had brought. My boys, along with Nancy and Jenny's spouses, were just across the hall in Miles's study talking. From where I stood I could hear their conversation—they were discussing my future. Ethan and Andrew wanted me to sell the house and move in with one of them, while Charlie and the others wanted me to stay here. What did I want? I looked around the large foyer, at the wood staircase with its carved banister, the tall ceiling. I then looked back into the formal dining room, where the women were finishing up, with its large mahogany table and fancy chandelier hanging above, the wall covering and matching curtains . . . The room was outdated—the entire house was—though it was still just as fancy as it was the first time I stepped into this house. I remember that day like it was yesterday. I could have changed the décor years ago—Catherine wouldn't have minded, even when she was still alive. But I never wanted to. This was her home. It had been in the family for years, and yes, even though it was my home too, and it had been for many, many years now, I couldn't imagine changing the décor. Especially not at my age, but even years prior. It would be almost like erasing the memory of Catherine. I reached out and touched the banister. I couldn't imagine living anywhere else . . . and yet to live here in this big house all alone . . . Could I? Should I? Even though Jenny and her husband lived just down the road, they too were getting up there in age and had been considering retiring, selling their part of the farm, and downsizing to a smaller newer home. Miles and I had not been able to care for the house on our own for several years now, and all our children helped in one way or another. Was it right for me to keep depending on them when they all had their own families to worry about? Did I want to stay here? Ever since our children had grown up and moved out, the big house seemed empty. Sure, we had company from time to time, and the house was always filled on holidays with grandchildren and then great-grandchildren. Still, most of the time it was just Miles and I . . . and now, with Miles gone . . . tears fell down my face yet again. With my tears still falling, I removed my hand from the banister then looked at the pictures that adorned the walls in the long hall. Pictures of our life together. I reached out and touched the black and white photo of Miles and me on our wedding day, smiling as I did so. It was taken while we stood on the front steps of his church. We weren't even looking at the camera—we were looking at each other, huge smiles on our faces. I wore a white dress just like I had always dreamed of. It had been Catherine's wedding gown originally. She and I had altered it, changed it up a little, making it new for me. Nancy and Jenny both wore the dress when they were married, and even a couple of my granddaughters. Miles . . . oh, Miles . . . he was so handsome in his suit. The first time I saw him, I was instantly attracted to him. How I wished I could touch him just once more. Taking my hand back, I slowly walked down the hall, looking at all my pictures. Pictures of our family over the years as it expanded— the things we had done and the places we had traveled. The further down the hall I walked, the more current the pictures became, changing from black and white to color. The hairstyles changed, the clothing changed, and even the people changed. The last several pictures were those of our great-grandchildren. How blessed Miles and I were. Each member of this family was a precious gift from God. I came to the end of the hall and entered the family room. When I had first moved into the house, this room did not exist. It was an addition that Miles built himself in 1973. I remember questioning him the entire time he was building it. The house was already large, and I didn't think we needed the extra space, but Miles went on ahead and built it anyway. And it was a good thing too because it was the only room in the house large enough to hold the entire family we when we all got together. I looked over at the empty chair sitting by the fireplace . . . his empty chair. "Oh, Lord," I whispered. "I knew I would miss him, but you did not tell me how much it would hurt." I then pictured Christ on the cross, and I knew the hurt I was feeling at this moment was nothing like the pain God the father felt as he watched his son being crucified for my sins. Nor was my pain anything close to the pain Jesus felt while he was beaten then nailed to that cross. I made my way over to Miles's chair and slowly sat. I could smell him. It was more than a scent, though—it was as if I could sense his presence, and it instantly brought me comfort. Small gifts. "Thank you, Lord," I whispered as I ran my hand over the worn arms of the chair.

I smiled as I thought about Miles and me. It was a miracle that we were even married . . . it was God who had brought us together, and I couldn't imagine where I would be today if he hadn't done so. Jenny entered the room and stopped short when she saw me sitting in her father's chair. I reached out my hand to her, and she came over and knelt, placing her head on my knees like she was a small child once again. I gently stroked her hair as she cried. Slowly, one by one, all my children and their spouses entered the family room. "I'm sorry, Mama," Jenny said as she lifted her head off my lap and wiped her tears.

"There's nothing for you to apologize about, baby," I said as I gently stroked her cheek. "It's alright to cry. We all miss your daddy."

She nodded, tears still falling. How I wanted to take her pain. I wished I could take all the pain from my children. But I knew I could not. That was a lesson I had learned years ago. My children were not really mine . . . not to keep anyway. God gave them to me for a season . . . the hardest thing to do as a parent is to let them go, let them experience life, both the good and the bad. "Mama, would you like us to stay here with you for a while?" Charlie asked. "'Cause if you want to be alone, we can all leave."

I looked over at the clock that sat on the mantel. It was just past three in the afternoon. "Please stay," I replied as I was not quite ready to be alone just yet.

"Of course we will, Mama," Jenny said, taking my hand in hers.

"Grandma, what's this?"

I looked over at my granddaughter Eva as she entered the family room carrying something in her hands. "Bring it here, darling, so I can see what it is you have," I said.

As she neared, I sucked in my breath. In her hands, she carried a tin box. A box I had not seen in years. At one time, it was shiny and black and had tiny yellow flowers painted on it. Now it was faded, scratched, and dented. The tin was now almost eighty years old—it was old like me. "I found it in the hall closet," Eva said as she handed me the tin.

I tried to open the lid, but it was stuck tight. "Here, let me help, Mama," Jenny said, taking the box from my hands. I watched with anticipation as she pried open the lid . . . It took her a minute, but finally she was able to open it. "Looks like junk," she stated as she looked inside.

Junk, I thought as I reached out and took the tin from her. *Junk! This was my life, and at one time, these were my treasures, and my daughter was calling this junk?* I looked down. Well, I could see how one might mistake this as junk. Unless they understood the story behind each item, then yes, one could easily mistake it as junk. Reaching in, I first pulled out a ribbon. A pale, faded, brittle ribbon that had once been bright red, shiny, and smooth. I could remember rubbing my fingers over the ribbon as a child, thinking of my mother while trying to picture her wearing this very ribbon in her hair. Dropping the ribbon back into the tin, I picked up a button. It, too, was old and faded, where it had once been shiny and silver with tiny engraved flowers around its edges. Flowers like one would place over a grave . . . how suiting. Next, I picked up the stack of letters with an old black and white photo on top, all held together by a rubber band. *Eric*, I thought. *How long has it been since we said goodbye?*

"Who is that man, Grandma?" Eva asked from her position, now standing behind the chair.

"He was my brother," I replied.

"The one killed in World War Two?" Nancy asked as she, too, was now huddled close, curious about the box.

"Yes."

"He was very handsome," Eva said.

"Yes, he was a very handsome young man," I agreed, smiling as I looked at his picture.

I did not cry—I hadn't cried for him in years—but I still missed him greatly. I often thought of Eric, what he would have done with his life if he had lived. It was funny looking at this old picture, because I realized for the first time just how much Eric looked like our father. I never recognized the resemblance until just now. I set the stack of letters in my lap then picked up the bus ticket. A one-way ticket that had changed my life forever. Setting the letters and the ticket back into the tin, I then picked up a key. The key was once shiny and gold, but it too was now faded, looking more bronze than it did gold. I looked up at Nancy . . . it was bittersweet, for although this key held many wonderful memories, it also held memories I would rather forget. Next, I picked up a stack of postcards. Just like the letters, they were held together by a rubber band. Without the key, I would not have these postcards, nor would I have Nancy. I set the postcards and the key into my lap then picked up the shell. It was about the size of a plum, rounded, shiny, and smooth. I had looked it up once years back at the library. It was called a tiger cowrie. It was tan with brown spots all over the top, but the flip side was cream with a bit of light lavender. It was the only thing in my tin that still looked new. It was beautiful. Which was ironic because this shell represented the darkest part of my life. Yet it was also a representation of how even in our sin, God still reigns supreme. How he uses the mess we have made of our lives for his purposes. I looked at my son, Ethan. From an early age, he had heart for God. When he was just seventeen, he left home and became a missionary in South America. It was there while on the mission field that he met his sweet wife, Maria. God used a man whose earthly father never claimed him to help thousands of children who also never knew their earthly fathers. Ethan and Maria had started an orphanage. They both loved children. Not only did they have five of their own, but they adopted three, and they considered all the children who passed through the doors of the orphanage to be theirs. Ethan just recently retired, and now his youngest son and his new wife were running the orphanage. He and Maria still lived in South America about eight months out of the year—I knew he would never truly 'retire.' I smiled as I thought of God's goodness. Had Miles not come into my life, then Ethan himself would have had no earthly father, nor would Nancy. For she, too, had been cut off from any relationship she might have had with her earthly father. I looked down at the very last item in my box—a small piece of newspaper, an ad for help. The ad that led me to Miles . . . The paper was yellowed, and I could tell it was very fragile, so I didn't bother to pick it up for fear of damaging it. I placed the shell, the key, and the postcards back inside as memories of my past flooded my mind. I had not thought about these things in years, and now suddenly the memories were back. Back and clear, playing like a movie as if it had just happened yesterday. I looked up at my all my children and their spouses. They were all sitting, silently watching, not a one of them was on their cell phone as often was the case. "Will you tell us about these things, Grandma?" Eva asked, breaking the silence in the room.

"Yes, Mother," Jenny said. "What are all these things?"

NO! I thought ... I couldn't... these were memories I had suppressed. Memories of my past ... In fact, it seemed as if the girl who saved all these things was gone, that it had been another person, another life.

Tell them, a small voice said to me.

No, Father, I can't ... my children, they don't know ... especially Nancy and Ethan, they can't know the truth ... my past ... they can't know ...

Tell them ... they need to know.

"Mama, are you alright?" Charlie asked.

I nodded. I was fine. I just didn't want to tell my children my story, but who was I to argue with God? So I took a deep breath as I picked up the faded ribbon with its frayed edges once again.

ONE

<u>July 1939</u>

Entering my bedroom, I shut the door, set the lock, then rushed over to my bed where I pulled out my black tin box with its floral design from its hiding place underneath. It was Christmas when we received the tin from our neighbor Mrs. Wilson, who lived just down the lane. Ever since Mama died five years ago, Mrs. Wilson would come and check in with us from time to time. And every Christmas she brought our family a small treat. It was different every year. One year it was a basket of canned goods, another year Mrs. Wilson had knitted all of us children scarves, and yet another year we received a stocking full of candy. This past Christmas, however, she gave us a tin full of cookies. After the cookies were eaten, my sister Lillian and I fought over who was going to keep the box. I was older, so naturally I won the argument, and the box was now mine. I kept my treasures hidden inside . . . or should I say treasure. For the only thing inside my tin was a red ribbon. Sitting on my bed, I pulled the lid off the tin then took hold of the ribbon. I ran my fingers over the soft silk, trying to remember what Mama looked like. This was her ribbon, and she only wore it on special occasions, like when we went to church. Papa didn't like church—he did not even like when Mama went—so we did not go often. In fact, now that Mama was gone, we didn't go to church at all, but when she was alive, we went every Christmas and Easter. Mama would make a fuss, making sure we were all bathed with our hair done and that we were dressed nicely too. And by nicely, I mean that our clothes were clean 'cause I never did have anything "nice." I owned two dresses. One was a blue calico and the other a floral print. Both had three buttons at the top, short sleeves, and came down to my knees. The floral print dress had a white collar around the neckline, making it just a bit fancier. However, both dresses were worn, almost thin, and they had been patched several times already. I lay back on my bed, looking up at the ceiling as I remembered the last time I had gone to church with Mama. It was Easter, and I was wearing a brown dress that my younger sister Helen now wore. That day, I saw girl about my age who was wearing a fancy yellow dress. Her dress had pleats running down the front as well as four shiny gold buttons and navy blue decorative trim along both the collar and sleeves. It was magnificent. She even wore matching yellow socks and had shiny black shoes. I was wearing my older brother's boots that day because it was the only pair of shoes we owned that fit me. They were way too big for me, chunky and hard to walk in. I wanted to go barefooted to church—I went barefooted every other day of the year—but despite my protest, Mama wouldn't allow it. She said she wouldn't allow any of us children to walk into God's house unless we were respectable. Seeing that girl dressed all fancy that day, it was the first time I realized just how poor we actually were. I envied that girl, I wanted to look pretty like her. My brother Eric somehow knew what I was thinking because he told me that I was much prettier than that girl. That I could have shown up to church wearing nothing but a flour sack and I would still be the prettiest girl there. Even at that young age, I knew he was just trying to make me feel better. So I was glad when we never returned to church. I never did like the way people looked at us when we were in town. I might have been a small child, but I saw how people stared at us and whispered. How they crossed the street so they didn't have to pass us on the sidewalk. Almost as if they were worried that being poor was an illness one could catch. Living out here on the farm, we were secluded, and I rarely ever had to see any other kids aside from my siblings. The only time we ever went to town was when Mama took us to church. Eric and Jeremy went to town on occasion with Papa, but he never took any of the rest of us. And we never went to school cause Papa said we didn't need any learning, that we needed to work. When Mama was alive, she taught

Eric, Jeremy, and I how to read and write, but that, too, stopped when she died. Still lying on my back, I began wrapping the ribbon around and around my finger, then unwrapping it and wrapping it around my finger again, all while trying to remember Mama's face. I couldn't do it . . . I knew she was pretty . . . beautiful with dark hair and blue eyes. And I remembered she always wore a smile on her face. But I could not remember her features . . . they had faded. I didn't know if it was because I was so young when she died or due to the passing of time. How I wished I had a picture of her, but we had none. Papa said pictures were a waste of time and money. I may not have had a picture, but at least I had her ribbon—well, a part of it. My sister Lillian and I fought over Mama's ribbon after she died, so our brother Eric cut it in half to stop our bickering. Had it not been cut, I could have worn it in my hair, just like Mama. But now it was too short. Still, it was part of Mama, and all I had to remember her by, so I treasured it. Lillian lost her half over a year ago. I kept mine hidden, safe. I didn't want her to find it and lose mine too. I stopped wrapping the ribbon around my finger and held it to my chest, close to my heart. I missed my mama. We all did . . . even Papa, though he never said. I knew he missed her 'cause it was after she died that he began to drink in excess and gamble too. Hearing thunder, I sat up and looked out the window. The sky that had been bright blue just minutes ago was now a dark gray. "The laundry," I whispered to myself as I placed the ribbon back inside the tin then popped on the lid. I quickly stood from the bed and shoved my box back underneath it so that my sisters wouldn't find it, then I ran over to the door, unlocked it, and ran from my room. Down the hall, down the steps, then down another long hall, and out the back door. "Lillian," I shouted to her across the yard, "come help me!" Grabbing a basket, I ran over to the clothesline. The storm was coming fast. Everything on the line was blowing in the wind. Setting the large basket down, I quickly began to pull the clothespins off a pair of my papa's pants, throwing both the pins and his pants into the basket. I then began pulling the pins off a sheet. "Hurry, Lillian!" I said as she joined me. Minutes later, I felt a raindrop on my arm, then another. I pulled a shirt off the line and threw it into the basket as Lillian threw in another sheet. There were still a handful of items on the line. The wind blew my hair into my face as we worked quickly to remove everything. Just as we finished, the sky opened up, and the rain poured down. Lillian and I each grabbed a handle on the basket and ran for the house. Once under cover of the porch, I looked down. The shirt on top was wet, but upon further inspection, I was relieved to find everything else was dry. I laid the wet shirt over the back of a chair then stood for a moment watching the rain, listening as it fell onto the tin roof. I always liked the clinking sound the rain made as it hit the roof—it was peaceful. Lightning flashed, followed by rolling thunder. From where Lillian and I stood on the back porch, I could see Papa and the boys running toward the barn for cover. I knew as they waited for the storm to pass they would be doing chores in the barn. The work never ended. There was always something to be done, even in the winter when things did slow down a bit. The animals still needed to be tended to, there was mending and other such chores that I did not have time for other times of the year . . . and meals. It was my job to prepare all our meals. "Come on, Lillian," I said. "Help me get this basket inside and put away, and then we can start dinner."

***

I pulled the potatoes out of the oven. Feeling the heat through the hot pads, I quickly set the bowl on the table. I then grabbed the plate of sliced tomatoes as well as a loaf of bread and set them on the table as well. Just then, the kitchen door swung open as the rest of the family entered the house. "Oh no you don't," I said as they immediately began taking their seats around the kitchen table. "You wash first!"

"Already washed," Eric said, holding up his hands. "We all did."

"Where? In the water trough?"

"Of course. Where else would we wash?" he replied with a serious face.

"Eric!" I said, voice raised.

"We washed at the water pump, silly," he said, now laughing as he sat at the table next to Jeremy.

There were eight of us children. At fourteen, I was the eldest girl. Eric, who was seventeen, was the eldest of us all. After me came Jeremy who was twelve, Lillian eleven, Helen nine, Danny and Brad, the twins who were seven, and the youngest was Michael. He was five. Mama had died just a few months after having Mike.

"Danny, be careful," I said as I placed the pitcher of milk on the table and noticed he was reaching out for the potatoes. "That's hot!" Danny pulled his hand away from the bowl and I grabbed a spoon, scooping some potatoes onto his plate. I then did the same for Brad. "See the steam?" I asked. The boys nodded. "I just pulled them potatoes out of the oven. They're very hot. Now be patient."

"Do we have any butter?" Eric asked.

"Yes," I replied as I spun around and grabbed the crock of butter off a shelf. "You need to be patient as well, I said as I set the butter down in front of Eric's plate. "I wasn't quite finished setting the table when you all waltzed in here and began to help yourself."

"Sorry," he replied with a sly smile as he began to butter his bread.

"Lillian!" I shouted as I plated Mike's food. "Dinner is ready!" Lillian entered the kitchen seconds later and took a seat at the table as I was pouring milk for Mike and the twins. The others were all old enough to serve themselves. "Where's Papa?" I asked when I realized he was not with us.

"Out," Eric replied. I gave him a surprised look . . . Papa never left to go drinking and gambling until after dinner. "He's at Frank's place," he said, clarifying. "Frank came by earlier and asked for help . . . having trouble with his tractor again."

***

I was standing at the kitchen sink washing the dinner dishes when Papa returned home that evening. I watched as his truck drove up the drive past the kitchen window. I listened as the engine shut off, and moments later the kitchen door swung open and he entered the house. Without a word, he sat at the table. I quickly dried my hands on the towel then grabbed his dinner plate off the counter. Removing the cloth that was covering the tomatoes and bread, I set the plate before him, walked over to the oven, and removed the bowl that held the potatoes. I scooped the remainder of them onto his plate. Then, grabbing a fork from the pile of just washed silverware, I held it out to him. He just looked at me. In fact, ever since he'd sat at the table, Papa had been watching me closely, and I wasn't sure why. He was a quiet man, but still, something was different tonight. "How old are you, Anne?" he asked as he took the fork from my hand.

"Fourteen," I replied, surprised that my papa didn't know my age.

"Fourteen already," he said. I nodded, just staring at my papa as he continued to look at me. "You remind me of her."

Once again, I nodded. People often told me that I looked like my mother. I didn't mind 'cause what little I did remember of my mother was that she was a stunning beauty. Still, to hear my papa speak of her . . . he never spoke of her. What was wrong with him? He wasn't drunk—I knew that much. "Do you want some coffee," I asked nervously.

"If we got it," he answered. I grabbed the coffee pot off the stove, glad I had thought to make a pot. He was still watching me as I poured the hot liquid into a mug. I set the mug on the table before him then turned my back to him and continued washing the dishes. "Frank was asking about you today," he said after several minutes had passed. I didn't say anything because I didn't know what to say. Frank was a friend of Papa's even though he was several years younger. Frank was in his mid-twenties, and Papa was thirty-nine. I'm not even sure where the two men met, though I assume it involved drinking, gambling, or perhaps both. When I finished washing the dishes, I turned around to find my father still watching me. I looked down at my feet, feeling awkward. Hearing Papa's chair slide across the floor a few seconds later, I looked back up. He grabbed his plate up off the table and handed it to me. "Dinner was good," he said. "Thank you." I nodded, wondering if Papa was ill. He never thanked us for anything, especially if it was our job and we were expected to do it. "See you in the morning," he said as he placed his hat on his head and walked out the door. Seconds later, I heard his truck start up, and he was gone . . . gone to drink and gamble.

***

I had just finished setting breakfast on the table when I saw Frank's truck pull into the drive. I grabbed another plate, assuming he was going to join us as he often did when he came around. Adjusting a few plates, I set another place just as all the kids came running into the kitchen. "Eggs and potatoes again?" Helen complained.

"Sit down and just be thankful you even have food to eat," I replied.

Helen did as she was told but not before giving me a sassy face. "Hey," Eric said, gently popping the back of Helen's head. "If you don't shape up, then you can go without breakfast."

"You are not my papa," she said under her breath.

Eric opened his mouth to speak, but then the door to the kitchen swung open, and Frank entered the house. Still standing by the door, he removed his hat and held it in his hands. "You're here earlier than I expected," Papa said as he took his seat at the table.

"I've come to collect the payment we agreed upon," Frank replied.

"Please join us for breakfast," my father said as he grabbed the bowl of scrambled eggs.

"Thank you, but I'd rather collect and be on my way."

My father poured a large amount of eggs onto his plate then handed the bowl to Eric before he locked eyes with Frank. "I'll give you what we agreed upon, but you'll have to wait. Now please join us for breakfast. I insist."

Frank nodded then walked to the table, taking one of the two empty seats. Papa obviously owed Frank money—it wasn't the first time. Still, Papa was a large man and very intimidating, so even though he was the one in debt, Frank was the one submitting right now. I grabbed the coffee pot and filled Papa's mug, then Eric's, then Frank's.

"You're awfully pretty today, Anne," Frank said, placing his hand on my arm.

I pulled my arm away. Frank was not by any means unattractive. In fact, he was quite handsome . . . still, he was old, much older than me. And besides, I never did like him. There was something about him that gave me an odd feeling whenever he was around. I was making my way toward the stove to set the coffee pot down when my father held out his mug. I refilled his cup, and when I was finished, he grabbed my arm, pulling me close, and he whispered in my ear, "Don't be rude to our guest." He released me, and I nodded, wondering what was going on. When did Papa ever care in the past how I treated Frank? Not that I was ever rude to any of Papa's friends or any other guest we might have. I set the coffeepot on the stove then turned around, realizing the only open seat was the one next to Frank. Reluctantly, I walked over and sat. Thankfully, Frank paid no more attention to me. He and Papa were talking about current events, mostly about what was going on overseas in Germany and the possibility of the United States going to war. Eric and Jeremy both joined in the conversation, but the rest of us sat quietly, just listening as we ate. I wondered if we did go to war, would Papa have to fight again? He fought in the last war, at least that's what Mama had told me, though Papa himself never talked about it. When breakfast was over, everyone dispersed as we all had chores to tend to. I stood from my seat and began collecting the dishes off the table to be washed. "Anne, you go pack your things. Lillian will clean the kitchen today," Papa said.

Lillian paused at the door, looking first at me then at Papa. She had a confused look on her face. I too was confused.

"Pack my things?" I asked as I set the plates I currently held back onto the table.

"Just do as I ask!" Papa yelled as he slammed his fist on the table.

I nodded as I quickly untied the apron from around my waist. I knew better than to question my papa, but I wasn't questioning him . . . not really. I didn't know what he meant by pack my things. I looked over at Lillian, who was holding back tears. She often cried when Papa yelled even if she was not the one he was angry with. Lillian had always been tenderhearted. "It's alright," I whispered, forcing a smile as I handed the apron to her. "Don't cry. Everything will be alright."

I then quickly left the room, still very confused. Pack my things . . . pack my things . . . was my father sending me away? If so, where was I going? And why? I entered the room I shared with my sisters, walked over to the dresser, and pulled open the top drawer that held all my things—my other dress, my nightgown, and a few undergarments. All of them worn, patched, and stained, but all I had. I picked everything up and placed it all on the bed. I had no valise or suitcase to put my belongings in, so I laid out my nightgown and rolled up everything else into it. Then, remembering my tin, I fell to my knees and fetched it out from under the bed. With the tin in my hands, I picked up my rolled-up nightgown with all my belongings. Holding everything to my chest, I looked around my room. The wallpaper was faded and torn in many places. The windows' sheer curtains were threadbare and frayed at the ends. There was a bed with an old patchwork quilt on it, a nightstand with an oil lamp sitting atop it, and a dresser. That was it . . . nothing fancy, nothing nice, but it was all I knew. I had been born in this house. Now where was I going? Would I be back? I took one last look around my room then nervously made my way back downstairs and back into the kitchen. "Are you ready to go?" Frank asked from where he now stood by the door.

Go? I thought. *Why was I going with Frank?* I looked at Papa, who now stood by the stove with a cup of coffee in his hands.

"You're going with Frank," he said. Lillian dropped the plate she was washing, and it hit the floor shattering into several pieces.

Then before I realized what I was doing, I shook my head and spoke. "No."

"Dammit girl," Papa said as he slammed his coffee mug down on the table, causing some of the coffee to spill out. He took two large strides toward me, grabbed hold of my arm, and pulled me toward the back door. "I did not raise you to be so defiant," he said angrily as he pushed Frank out of the way and dragged me outside.

"Papa, no!" I heard Lillian yell.

Papa stopped walking and turned around. I too turned around. Lillian was standing on the bottom step. "Get back inside!" he yelled to her.

"No!" Lillian shouted. My jaw dropped, and I stared at her, shocked. Papa did the same . . . never had she ever spoken to him in such a manner. "Papa, please don't make Anne go." She was crying, and her voice was soft once again.

"This isn't your business, girl. You get back into the house right now!" Papa was angry. I could tell by his tone. Lillian stood. She didn't speak, but she didn't move, either. "Now, Lillian," Papa yelled, "or your backside will be so sore you won't be able to sit for days when I get done with you!"

With her lip quivering and more tears falling from her eyes, Lillian turned and ran back into the house. I was glad she did for I knew Papa would make good on his promise if she had chosen to disobey. Then once again, he began to drag me through the yard toward the driveway where Frank's truck was parked. By now, the rest of my siblings were standing in the yard, all watching and wondering what was going on. They were scared—I could see it in their faces. I was scared too. "Papa, please," I cried as he squeezed my arm tightly. "You're hurting me." Stopping just feet from Frank's truck, he released me. "Please, Papa . . . I don't understand."

"Get in," he said, opening the door to Frank's truck.

It was then that Eric ran over. "Papa, what's going on?"

"Nothing. Now go back out to the barn and get your chores done."

"No," Eric said, standing his ground. "Not until you tell me what's going on."

Papa looked at me and then at Eric before speaking. "I owe Frank money . . . lots of money . . . I was going to lose the house. I tried to pay him back . . . but I can't, so he agreed to take your sister for payment."

"Me?" I whispered in disbelief.

"Yes, you're his wife now, so get into the truck," Papa said, looking at me once again.

"No, you can't do this!" Eric protested.

"I'm her father, not you!" Papa yelled.

I noticed then that Papa was clenching his fists. I was afraid he was going to hit Eric. "She's fourteen, Papa! You can't give her to Frank."

I flinched as Papa grabbed the front of Eric's overalls. "You want to tell me what I can and cannot do?" he yelled. "You are my son, and you will do as I say, just like Anne will do as I say because she is my daughter."

He then released Eric with such force that Eric stumbled and fell. "I won't let you do this, Papa!" Eric yelled as he jumped to his feet.

"Another word from you, and you'll be sorry! I might be older, but I'm bigger and stronger than you, son." Papa and Eric stared each other down for what seemed like forever, though I knew it was just minutes. I wanted Eric to fight for me . . . and I could tell he wanted to. But when he finally looked away from Papa, I was also relieved because I knew Papa would have gotten the best of him. "Get in the truck, Anne," Papa said, turning his attention back to me once again.

"Wait!" Eric said as he pushed past Papa and embraced me. "I'm sorry," he whispered.

My eyes filled with tears as he held me for a long minute. Eric had always looked out for me, more so than he did anyone else. We were close, always had been. He released me and wiped my tears before taking a step back. I now saw Frank—he stood just several feet away with a smile on his face. I didn't want to get into the truck. I didn't want to be Frank's wife, but I knew I couldn't disobey Papa.

So numbly, I climbed in and sat holding all my possessions in my lap. Papa then shut the door, and I watched through the window as he and Frank exchanged a few words. Eric turned his back and started for the barn. And though it felt as if he was abandoning me, I knew deep down inside he wasn't. I knew he couldn't bear to watch me leave. Minutes later, Frank walked around and entered the truck. Without a word, he started the engine. I placed the palm of my right hand on the window as I stared out at my papa. He was staring back, though his face was stone, showing no emotion whatsoever. How could he do this? How could he give me away? His own daughter? The truck began to move, and it was only after my house was no longer in sight that I turned my head to look at Frank. His eyes were fixed on the road ahead.

"Are we going to the church?" I asked in just above a whisper.

"Church?" he asked.

I could hear the confusion in his voice. "Yes, to get married. Aren't we supposed to go to church to be married?"

Frank glanced at me, smiling. "No need."

"But . . . I thought that when two people got married, they did so in a church."

"Not always," he replied.

I looked down at my belongings, still holding them tightly. I was disappointed. I had always wanted to get married in a church and wear a fancy white dress. I don't know why . . . I just always had ever since I had seen pictures of wedding gowns in a magazine that Mama once had. I was disappointed, and not just disappointed . . . I was frightened too. I didn't know what to expect. I didn't know how to be a wife. The two of us rode silently the rest of the way to Frank's house. I had never been to his house before, so I had no idea where we were going. When we entered our small town and drove right through, back into the country once again, I was even more disappointed. Wherever it was that Frank lived, it was too far to walk to Papa's, so I wouldn't see my family very often. About five miles outside of town, he turned off the dirt road onto a small dirt lane. As we did, we passed by a small white house with green shutters and a white picket fence, then farther down the lane we passed another house. This one was slightly larger than the first. Both houses were in good condition, clean and tidy. Our house was always clean—Lillian and I saw to that—but it was not in good condition. Papa didn't keep up with the repairs. The paint on our house had been peeling for years, and the shutters were hanging crooked or completely missing. In many places, the fence around our house had fallen or was missing boards. Eric tried to keep up with the repairs, but he was so busy helping Papa in the fields that the repairs just didn't get done. And it wasn't just the time. We never had any spare money . . . Papa spent it all drinking and gambling. There was never any money to buy paint or any other supplies needed to keep up with the repairs. Frank continued on for another half a mile then pulled into a long drive. I looked out my window as Frank got out of the truck. His house was not as large as my Papa's, but it was a lot nicer and well taken care of. I could tell it had recently been painted. It was yellow with white trim and black shutters. There was a porch that ran across the front of the house then wrapped around the side. Frank opened my door, and I stepped out of the truck, still clinging tightly to my belongings.

"Come on," he said.

I followed him up the steps and onto the front porch where he opened the front door and ushered me inside. I found myself standing in a small foyer. To my right was a parlor, and to my left was a dining room. Straight ahead, I saw part of a kitchen. The outside of the house was clean and tidy, but the inside was the complete opposite. It was filthy. There was dust, and there were cobwebs, and all sorts of things were out of place. I figured it was because there was no woman living here . . . at least until now.

"This way," Frank said, starting up the steps. I followed once again. At the top of the stairs, we passed a bedroom, and another, and then entered the room at the far end of the hall. There was a metal bed that was unmade with a nightstand on either side. A washstand, a dresser, and a chair sat in the corner near the window.

I looked down at my bare feet. I was standing on a braided rug. Once again, the room was dusty and disorderly, with clothing thrown all about. The house could be nice, much nicer than the home I grew up in, if it was clean. "You can put your things in here," Frank said as he pulled open one of the drawers in the dresser. He removed its contents, and I watched as he shoved everything into the drawer above. When he was finished, and the drawer was empty, he stepped aside. I walked over and deposited my things into the now empty drawer. He closed the drawer, and we stood silently just looking at one another. I didn't like the way he was looking at me. I was frightened, and I just wanted to go home. Reaching out, he touched my cheek. I stepped back immediately.

"No, you don't," he said, grabbing my arm and pulling me close. "You belong to me."

TWO

I woke the next morning to find the bed beside me empty. I was relieved to know that Frank was gone . . . at least for now. I sat up, clutching the sheet around my naked body as more tears fell down my face. I had cried myself to sleep, and now I was crying again. I had no idea what happened between a man and a woman . . . I had no idea anything happened before yesterday. I was in pain, I was sore, and the thought of Frank touching me like that again frightened me. I knew I couldn't stay in bed all day, so I stood, and then I noticed blood on the sheets. Dropping the sheet, I looked down between my legs. I didn't see anything, so I took my right hand and touched myself. When I pulled my hand back, I saw a little bit of blood on my fingers. I wasn't sure if I was having my monthly or if what Frank did to me caused me to bleed. 'Cause it hurt, it hurt bad. Would I bleed every time he touched me? I wished Mrs. Wilson was here so I could ask her. She was the one my father called the day I first bled. It was only a few months ago when it happened the first time. I was hysterical and, afraid I was dying, had locked myself in my room. Papa had Eric run down the lane and fetch Mrs. Wilson. After she calmed me down and helped me clean up, she explained to Lillian, Helen, and me what happened when a young lady became a woman. Lillian and Helen had not yet bled, but Mrs. Wilson must have figured it would save her a trip in the future. I walked over to the wash basin and cleaned myself up before getting dressed for the day. I then stripped the sheets off the bed to be washed.

"Anne!" I heard Frank call as I was making my way down the steps. I found him in the kitchen, sitting at the table with a mug of coffee and a plate of toast before him. "I let you sleep in today, but from now on, I expect you to get up early and have breakfast ready as well as a lunch pail packed for me."

I nodded. I was used to getting up early and making breakfast each morning. I was actually surprised when I had awakened this morning, realizing I had slept in.

"Sit," he said, pulling out the chair beside his. I dropped the soiled bedding onto the floor then slowly walked over to the table and sat. He smiled as he reached out, running his fingers through a lock of my hair. He placed his other hand on my leg, and I instantly stiffened. Leaning forward, he brushed his lips across mine. "I'll be back at six, and I expect dinner to be ready," he said after a quick kiss. I nodded my response as he stood from his chair, and I watched silently as he left.

As soon as the door slammed shut behind him, I wiped my lips with the back of my hand then sat listening, waiting to hear the sound of his truck starting. It didn't, so I stood and walked over to the door. Looking out the large window that was cut out in the door, I first saw his truck, and then I saw Frank . . . just as he disappeared into the barn. I should have known he wouldn't be leaving. He was a farmer like my papa. He would spend his day working the land, growing mostly tobacco and some corn. Suddenly overwhelmed with emotion, I fell to my knees crying. This was my life . . . Frank was my husband, and I was his wife. I had to obey him, and if he wanted to touch me, I had to allow it. Did my papa touch my mama in this way? I doubted he did . . . 'cause Mama was always happy, and if Papa touched her the way Frank touched me, I doubt Mama would have been happy.

***

September 1939

Kneeling in the vegetable garden, I was in the process of pulling out all the dead plants and throwing them into a wheelbarrow. I had harvested and canned all the vegetables I could and was now preparing the garden for winter. I looked up, wiping my brow. I could tell I swiped dirt across my face, but I didn't care. I was hot even though it wasn't hot outside. I wasn't feeling well—I hadn't felt well for several days. Still, the work had to be done, so here I was. Looking back down, I began to pull another dead plant from the ground, and as I did, something shiny caught my eye. Digging it out of the soil, I picked it up. The object was covered in dirt, so I brushed away the dirt and quickly realized it was a button. A very fancy button. It was the size of a dime, rounded with an intricate floral design carved into it. It was beautiful. I had never seen such a beautiful button before. I slipped it into the pocket of my apron and dug around, hoping to find a few more. Frank had just purchased some material for me to make a new dress, and if I could just find another button or two, I would definitely use them. Unfortunately, I couldn't find any more buttons. I was disappointed. Still, I had one. I continued to pull the dead plants for another few minutes, then stopped and stood. I needed a break, and I was thirsty. As I walked into the house, I put my hand into my apron pocket, fingering the button. Stopping at the back door, I wiped my bare feet on the rug, hoping to remove most of the dirt before I stepped inside. I had swept and mopped the kitchen floor earlier this morning, and I did not want to have to do so again if I could help it. Walking over to a cabinet, I removed a glass then picked up the pitcher of water that was sitting on the counter and poured myself a glass. As I drank, I looked out the window. I could see Frank in the distant field planting the winter wheat. I turned around so that my back was now to the window as I leaned against the sink. I had cleaned the house the first week I arrived and organized everything. It was nice and very comfortable, much nicer than the home I grew up in. The kitchen had yellow paneling up to a green chair rail, the same green the cabinets were painted. Above the paneling, the walls were papered—white with large yellow florals. The wood floor was painted a light gray. And the stove was my favorite ... it was gas. So easy to use compared to the wood burning stove Papa had. And the great thing was that it didn't heat the kitchen up like the wood burning stove did. At least in the summer that was good. Though I would probably miss the heat in the winter. The parlor, too, was nice. There were two sofas and a couple of side tables with oil lamps sitting atop doilies. There was a braided rug over the wood floor and a nice fireplace. There was even a small bookcase with a handful of books. I loved to read, but I didn't have any time to read, not yet. But once winter came, I was hoping to be able to read some. On top of the bookcase was a radio, Frank's radio. I had learned the hard way not to touch it. The dining room was nice too. It had a large table with six chairs around it, but we never ate there. We always took our meals out here in the kitchen. The entire house was nice. Frank told me he had purchased it from a widower several years back, which explained the womanly touches throughout. But despite how nice the house was, it did not reflect my marriage. Frank drank about as often as Papa did, but when Frank got drunk, he got violent. Setting my glass into the sink, I pushed back the collar of my dress, inspecting the large bruise I had on my right shoulder. My skin was a yellowish purple color. I received that one two days ago, and I had another bruise on my back I had gotten the day before. They were both still very sore. Hearing a knock on the door, I quickly pulled my dress back up to cover the bruise. I wondered who it could be. We had not had any guests in the months since I had lived here. I was hoping it was Eric coming for a visit, and maybe he brought Lillian too. I hadn't seen or heard from any of my family since the day I left home. 'Course it was a busy time of year, but I knew Eric would come to see me as soon as he could get away. Excitedly, I opened the door only to be disappointed when I saw a middle-aged woman standing on the porch holding a pie in her hands. She had bright red hair that was neatly done up. Green eyes and freckles across her nose and cheeks. Her dress was very nice, and she even wore a string of pearls around her neck. "Hello," she said, smiling. "I'm your neighbor down the lane. I live in the first house. My name is Mary, Mary Harper."

"Hello," I said shyly. "Please come in."

I stepped back, and Mary entered the house. "I'm looking for Frank's wife . . . Anne, I believe that's her name?"

"I am Anne," I said as I shut the door.

"Oh," Mary's face showed surprise. "I . . . well . . . I guess I wasn't expecting you to be so young. Here, this is for you," she said, handing me a pie. "Cherry pie, last of the season."

"Thank you," I said as I took the pie from her. "I'll put this in the kitchen."

As I began to walk down the hall toward the kitchen, I could hear Mary's footsteps as she followed behind. "You have a very nice home, Anne. I've never been inside before."

"Thank you," I replied, setting the pie down on the counter. "Would you like something to drink?" I asked.

"Water would be wonderful," she said. I nodded then grabbed a clean glass from the cabinet. After I poured the water, I handed the glass to Mary. "So how long have you and Frank been married?" she asked after she had taken a drink.

"A little over two months."

"Two? I just found out four days ago," she said. "I'm sorry. I would have come by sooner had I known you were here."

I nodded, shyly smiling as I tucked a strand of stray hair behind my ear. I was nervous, not sure what to say or what to do . . . I had never entertained a lady before. Mrs. Nelson would come to our house, but somehow that was different. Suddenly I felt faint. I placed my hand on the counter to steady myself as the room began to spin. Slowly everything went black, and as I fell to the floor, I could hear Mary calling my name.

***

I opened my eyes, and it took me a few moments to realize I was lying in bed. "You gave us a fright," Mary said. I turned my head to see her sitting in a chair at my bedside. "How are you feeling?" she asked, smiling, as she wiped my forehead with a damp cloth

"I don't know . . . I feel strange," I whispered. "I haven't been feeling well for several days now."

"Well, I think you're going to be just fine. I think you just might be with child," she said, patting my arm.

"With child?" I said, wondering exactly what she meant by that.

"Yes, well, we'll find out soon enough. Frank went to my house to call the doctor. He should be arriving anytime. I'm glad I came over when I did. Who knows how long it would have been before Frank would have discovered you passed out on the kitchen floor?"

Just then, I heard the front door open, then voices. One was Frank's, and he was speaking to another man—the doctor, I assumed. Both their footsteps and voices became louder as they made their way up the stairs then down the hall. Seconds later, Frank stepped into the room, followed by the other man. The other man was older than Frank, but not elderly. He looked to be close to my father's age. He was dressed really nice, and he carried a bag in his right hand. I had never seen a doctor before, so I wasn't sure what to expect. We could never afford doctors. If one of us got sick, we cared for one other at home. The doctor stood at the foot of the bed looking at me, and then he looked at Frank.

"How old did you say your wife was?"

"She's sixteen . . . legal age to be wed," Frank said, though he was lying. I was still fourteen. My fifteenth birthday was still four months away.

The doctor stood looking at Frank a moment longer. I think perhaps he didn't believe him. "What's your name?" he asked as he approached my bedside.

"Anne," I whispered nervously as Mary stood and the doctor took her seat.

"I'm Daniel, Doctor Dan . . . has sort of a ring to it doesn't it?" I nodded, still very nervous, especially since I didn't know what to expect. "You have nothing to worry about, Anne," he said as he smiled and patted my arm. "I'm just going to ask you a few questions and then examine you so we can find out why you fainted." I nodded again. "Frank, if you will step out into the hall," Doctor Dan said. "I'll call for you when I am finished."

I was glad when Frank left the room, and I was even gladder that Mary stayed. Just like he said, Doctor Dan asked me several questions. Some very personal, and I was embarrassed to answer them, but Mary told me it was okay to tell the doctor, so I did. He then examined me, which was even more uncomfortable than answering his questions. "What happened to your arm?" he asked when he saw my bruise.

I was afraid Frank might hit me again if I told the truth. "I . . . I fell," I lied.

"And the bruise on your back?"

"I didn't realize I had a bruise on my back," I lied again. "It, too, must have happened when I fell."

His eyes locked with mine, and I wasn't sure if he believed me. I looked away, and he continued on with his examination, so I figured that perhaps he had believed my lie. Covering my legs with the sheet, I was glad when it was over. Doctor Dan then called Frank back into the room. "Your wife is definitely pregnant," he said after Frank entered.

"Pregnant?" Frank's face was one of shock. "But how is that possible?"

Doctor Dan gave Frank a look. "Surely you don't need me to explain . . . "

"No," Frank said, running his hands through his hair. "It's just . . . she's so young . . ."

"Yes, she is, and you should be ashamed of yourself," Doctor Dan said. He looked back at me. "You need to take it easy, Anne. Take lots of breaks throughout the day, rest when you can, drink lots of water, and eat well."

"Will this yucky feeling go away?" I asked.

"In time," he replied, smiling. "It's common for women to feel ill when they are first pregnant."

I looked over at Frank, who was now standing in front of the window looking out. Was he mad at me? I hoped he didn't think I did this on purpose. I wasn't even sure how it happened. I looked down at my flat belly. I remembered Mama being fat when she was pregnant with both the twins and Mike. "Mama was always fat when she was pregnant," I said. "How come I'm not fat?"

"Give it time, Anne," the doctor said, smiling. "Your belly will grow as the baby does. Right now, your baby is very tiny." He held his hand up showing me the baby's size. I couldn't imagine a baby being that tiny. "And you call me if you need anything," he said as he grabbed his bag off the foot of the bed. I nodded. "Frank, a word," he said as he walked out into the hall. I assumed Doctor Dan took Frank into the hall so they could speak privately, but Mary and I heard every word. "You hurt her again, and I will report you to the authorities, understand?" Doctor Dan was angry. I could tell by the tone of his voice. "Don't you dare lay a finger on her!"

"Well," Mary said, quickly shutting the door, "a baby . . . just as I thought," she said as she approached the bedside once again. "How exciting."

***

December 1939

Frank no longer hit me, he must have believed that Doctor Dan would do as he threatened. I was glad, though I wished the doctor would have told Frank not to touch me as well 'cause unfortunately that did not stop. The days passed, and eventually I began to feel better. I now had a small belly. I was definitely with child. I still didn't know how it happened, and thankfully Frank was not mad at me. He was actually excited, talking about "his son" from time to time, though I wasn't sure how he knew the baby was going to be a boy. Doctor Dan told me we had no way of knowing what the baby was going to be until after it was born. So I had picked out two names, one for a boy and another for a girl.

Hearing a knock on the door, I set the mending aside. As I stood from my place on the sofa and made my way to the front door, I wondered who it could be. It was a cold day, and it had been raining since the early hours of the morning. If it got much colder, the roads would all be ice. I opened the door.

"Eric," I said, smiling, as I threw my arms around him.

"Anne," he replied, wrapping his arms around me.

"Come in. It's freezing out here," I said moments later.

"Is Frank here?" he asked as he stepped inside and began to remove his jacket and hat. "I didn't see his truck."

"No, he ran to town," I replied as Eric hung his items on the coatrack. "Tea?" I asked.

"Yes, I would love some."

"Follow me to the kitchen," I said as I turned and made my way down the hall. It was only after I entered the kitchen that I realized Eric was not behind me. I peeked down the hall and saw him checking out the parlor first then the dining room. Still smiling, I filled the teapot with water then placed it on the stove. Hearing footsteps, I turned around just as Eric entered the kitchen. "It will be a few minutes before it's ready," I said.

"You have a really nice house, Anne," he said, looking at the kitchen. "I've been over here a couple times in the past, but I never came inside."

I nodded. The house was nice. I just wish I could say the same about my marriage. I would give this house up with all its comfort and conveniences in a heartbeat if I could return home. "Please sit." I motioned to the table.

As Eric pulled a chair and sat, I grabbed a plate of cookies I had just made that morning from the pie cabinet. "Mom's recipe?" he asked as I set the plate on the table.

"Of course," I replied, smiling once again.

He grabbed four cookies off the plate, and I stood watching him eat. In seconds, they were all gone. "Are you starving?"

"No . . . but we might as well be. Lillian can't cook very well."

I chuckled as I set two mugs on the table. "Well, cooking was never her strong suit. She'll learn." Eric grabbed two more cookies as I poured the tea. I set the pot back on the stove then grabbed a jar of honey and set it before Eric. I then sat in the chair beside his. "Other than the food, how are you all doing?" I asked. "I miss you."

He grabbed my hand and squeezed. "I miss you too. We all miss you. And we're managing. Papa . . . he drinks a lot more . . . I don't think he wanted to give you to Frank."

"But he did," I said as tears dropped from my eyes.

Reaching over, he wiped my tears away, looking at me with concern and tenderness. "How are you, Anne?"

"Pregnant."

"I know. Besides the fact that you're showing, Frank told Papa several weeks ago. I wanted to come visit you sooner, much sooner. I'm sorry I didn't, but I couldn't get away."

"I know . . . I understand. I've been busy too," I said as I wrapped my hands around the warm mug. "How is Lillian doing?"

"Honestly . . . she's struggling without you," he replied. "I wanted to bring her with me today, but Papa wanted her home to help with the young'uns."

"Perhaps next time," I said. He nodded, and we both sat silently sipping our tea. "I'm scared," I whispered after several minutes passed.

"You will be a great mother, Anne. You raised the twins and Mike practically on your own."

"That's not what frightens me, Eric . . . it's the birth. I have no idea what to expect."

He smiled. "Nor do I, but if Mama could do it, I know you can."

I smiled. It was so good to see him. It had been too long. "Will you stay for dinner, Eric?" I asked.

"Gladly. A decent meal would do me wonders."

***

January 1940

I woke with intense cramps. Sitting up, I placed my hand on my belly. I was in pain, severe pain. "Frank," I whispered, frightened as the cramping intensified. "Frank," I whispered again, this time reaching out and touching his arm when he didn't respond the first time.

"You surprise me, Anne," he said, rolling over still half asleep. "I thought you would never ask."

"Frank, no!" I cried out. "Something is wrong."

"Do be quiet, Anne," he said as he laid me down.

"Please, Frank," I yelled as he straddled me.

"You little . . ." he grabbed the front of my nightgown. "You don't tell me what to do!"

I braced myself, waiting for him to strike me, but he didn't. Instead he reached down, lifting my nightgown. *Not now* I thought. *Not this . . . I'm in way too much pain.* Then suddenly he released me, and I could hear him shuffling about the room in the dark.

I sat up, crying out from the pain. Seconds later, the room illuminated as the oil lamp was lit. I looked down and gasped. Blood! There was blood everywhere. Frightened, I looked up at Frank. "What's wrong?" I cried out. He didn't answer me. He just stared at me, and I couldn't tell if he was angry or afraid. Then, without a word, he grabbed his pants off the chair and quickly stepped into them. Grabbing his shirt he quickly put it on, leaving the room before it was completely buttoned. "Frank!" I called out.

Once again, he didn't answer me. I listened to his footsteps as he ran down the stairs. I heard the front door open then slam shut, and then seconds later, I heard him trying to start the truck. It took several tries before the engine turned, and then I could hear the truck as it drove off down the gravel drive. Where was he going? Was he going down the lane to the Harpers? They had a phone in their house. Was he going to call the doctor? Or was he going off to drink? Surely he wasn't going off to drink . . . not now. I looked down once again. Red . . . so much blood . . . and the pain. I didn't know what to do. So I clutched my stomach, still in pain, and I cried. I was afraid, and I was alone.

THREE

March 1942

Just over two years had passed since I lost my baby. I sat by the simple gravestone that read *Baby of Anne and Frank Jones*, holding the button I had found the day I discovered I was pregnant. It was silly, but it was the only real thing I could hold on to that reminded me of my baby. I often wondered if my baby had been a boy or a girl. I wish I knew . . . I wanted so desperately to give my child a name. As I stood to my feet, I wiped my tears away. No matter how much time passed, my heart ached for my loss. A cold breeze blew past, and I pulled my sweater tightly around me then started back toward the house. We had buried our baby under the large black walnut tree that grew several yards behind the barn. Mama was buried in the cemetery behind the church, but I didn't want our child to be buried there. I hardly ever went to town, and with my baby buried here on our property, I could visit anytime I wished. Frank and I did not have any other children, nor had I been pregnant since that first time. At seventeen, I was beginning to wonder if I could even have children. Maybe something had happened, and I was to be barren. Perhaps it was a good thing that I had no children 'cause after I lost the baby, Frank began to hit me again. Maybe he would hit our babies too.

As I neared the house, a truck pulled into the drive. It was Eric. He had come to say goodbye. We were officially at war. Just a few months earlier, the Japanese attacked Pearl Harbor. I ain't never heard of the place before that day in December. Nor did I know anything about Japan. But after it happened, it was all over the news. Frank had left a week ago. I was glad he was gone—I didn't miss him at all. Eric, on the other hand . . . I would miss him. He stepped out of the truck, and seeing him in his uniform, it hit me how real this was. He was really leaving. I couldn't help but smile as he was so handsome in his uniform. At twenty, he had already broken the hearts of a few local girls.

"What are you doing out here on a cold day like this?" he asked, coming to my side. "You're going to get sick."

"I'm fine," I replied. "I just needed some fresh air."

We linked our arms and silently walked back into the warm house, entering into the kitchen via the backdoor.

"How are you managing on your own?" Eric asked as he removed his hat.

"I'm managing just fine."

"I know Frank has only been gone a week, but you should think about moving back home with Papa while he's away. You won't be able to take care of the farm by yourself, Anne."

"Frank hired some local boys to do the heavy work. I can take care of the animals and the house. I'll be fine, Eric. Don't worry about me." He nodded. "Will you write?" I asked.

"Only if you promise to write me," he replied with a smile.

Eric, Jeremy, and I were the only children who could read and write. Mama made sure we could. I wasn't proficient, however. Even now I still struggled with big words and spelling. At one time I had tried to teach the younger children, but when Papa found out, he forbade it. "Of course I will," I said. "I want details . . . I want to know everything . . . I want to see the colors and taste the food. I want to experience it all."

"Maybe you should sign up and join me," he said, chuckling. "Then you could see the world for yourself."

"Well, we both know that's impossible," I replied, smiling. The thought of Eric traveling halfway across the world fascinated me. None of us had ever left this town in which we had been born, and now Eric was leaving, off to see places I could only dream of. Of course, the reality of it was that it was not a holiday . . . this was war. Papa was not called to this war…he was not only above the age of forty but also a widower with several young children still at home. Jeremy wanted to go, but he was only fifteen and had to wait another two years before he was allowed to enlist. I was glad he couldn't go 'cause hopefully by the time he was seventeen, this war would be over. "When do you leave?" I asked.

"I catch a bus in town at three."

I looked at the clock—it was eleven thirty. "Stay for lunch?"

"When have you ever had to convince me to stay for a meal, Anne?" he replied, smiling.

***

March 1943

A year had passed since I last saw Eric. In the first letter he wrote to me shortly after he left, he had enclosed a picture of him in his uniform. I kept it in my tin along with all the letters he had written me over the past year. The button and the ribbon were still in my tin as well. Frank had written to me a few times, but I never once responded. I did not miss him, not one bit. The war continued on much longer than most of us had anticipated. Jeremy, too, was gone overseas. He left a month ago, days after he turned sixteen. A law had been passed that with parental permission, sixteen-year-olds could sign up, and Jeremy convinced Papa to let him go. The two boys Frank had hired to help here on the farm were both leaving next week. They told me so this morning. I would have to find more help. There was no way I could run this farm on my own. Mary's husband was gone as well. In fact, most of the men in our town were gone. Only young boys and old men remained. Many of the wives were now doing the jobs their husbands had once done. And it wasn't just here in our little town—it was everywhere. Times were hard, but for me . . . I preferred it this way. Sure, the war was an awful thing, and I wished it had never begun, that it would soon end, and all the men would return home. But I didn't miss Frank, and to be honest, I did not want him to return. It had been just over a year since the last time I had been beaten.

Eric and I wrote often, as often as we could. At first, his letters were full of optimism, and he described the places he went in such detail that I could close my eyes, and it was almost as if I was right there with him. But as time passed, the details were fewer and fewer. Mary came over several times a week and would bring papers when she did, in which we would read about the war. Sometimes I would go to her house in the evenings after my chores were done, and we would listen to the news on her radio. We had a radio here at the house—it was Frank's. Once, when we were first married, I was listening to a radio program when he came home drunk. He beat me black and blue, told me never again to touch his radio. I knew he wasn't here, that he was somewhere on the other side of the world, but for some reason, I was still scared. Thought for sure that if I even touched his radio, he would know . . . perhaps even show up out of nowhere and beat me again. I know it's silly, but I decided not to take the chance, so I just left it alone. I don't even bother to dust it.

After hearing about the war on the radio and reading about it in the newspaper, I knew why Eric's letters had changed. I could only imagine what he and the other men fighting over there were experiencing. I sometimes wondered when he returned home if he would be the same joyful person I knew. His latest letter had arrived just this morning, and I now held it in my hands. It had been several weeks since I had last received a letter, and I had waited all day to read it. Excited, I opened the envelope and pulled out the letter as I sat on the sofa.

> *Dearest Anne,*
>
> *I hope this letter finds you well. I am sorry for the delay in my writing. As you can imagine, things have been busy here. I'm on my way to Africa as I write this. Africa . . . can you imagine? I have already been to several countries in Europe, and now I will be going to Africa. Perhaps I shall see a lion! I do have exciting news . . . Jason, one of the guys in our unit, has been talking to us, and well, I'm not sure*

how to say this, so I'm just going to say it and hope I don't sound crazy. I'm in love . . . but it's not with a girl . . . at least not at this time. Perhaps someday when I return home. No, I have another love in my life. I have accepted Jesus into my heart to be my Lord and savior, and my life has completely changed. I have meaning and purpose, and I no longer fear death. Not that you knew I was fearful . . . but here, when death is a daily reality, it makes one start to question what really does happen after we die. Oh, I have so much more to tell you, but I'm running out light and paper, so it will have to wait until next time. Just know that I love you and most of all that God loves you. He loves you so much he sent his son to die for our sins. Nothing would please me more, Anne, than to know you belong to Him. His grace and peace are amazing! I can't wait to share more with you about what Christ has done in my life even though I have only known him for a short time.

Love always,

Eric

I folded the letter then just sat looking at it as I held it in my hands. I wasn't sure what I thought. I wasn't expecting Eric to write what he did. God had never been a huge part of our lives. Sure, I believed God existed, that he created the earth and everything on it. But he loved me? If he loved me, then why did he take my mama? Why did he allow my papa to drink and gamble and give me to Frank? Why did he take my baby? And what about this war and all the other wars of the past? What kind of loving God allowed these bad things to happen? No, God did not love me . . . Eric maybe, 'cause everyone who ever met Eric loved him . . . but God did not love me.

Hearing a truck pull into the drive, I looked out the window from was where I was sitting on the sofa in the parlor. It was Papa. I didn't think much of his visit as he came by from time to time to check on me ever since Frank had gone. I folded Eric's latest letter and placed it on top of all the others. Then, putting his picture on the very top, I wrapped a rubber band around the stack and placed it inside my tin. I set the tin on the sofa—I would put it up later—then stood and walked to the front door. No sooner had I stepped out onto the front porch than I shivered. It was a cold March day. I should have grabbed my sweater before coming out. As I made my way down the front steps, I noticed Papa was still sitting in his truck. When I neared the truck, he opened the door and stumbled out. He was drunk. What was he doing drunk at this time of the day?

"Papa, what are you doing here in your condition?" I asked.

He took a few steps toward me, speaking as he did. His speech was slurred, and he couldn't even walk straight. I was surprised he had been able to drive. With a bottle still in hand, he took a few more steps, then falling to his knees, he wrapped his arms around my waist. He was still mumbling something, and I still couldn't understand a word.

"Papa, come inside and lie down," I said, trying to pry his hands off me.

"No!" he shouted.

At least it sounded like he said no. He reached into his pocket and a minute later produced a letter which he placed into my hand. Then, falling onto his backside, he put the bottle to his mouth and took a long swig. I took a few steps back, distancing myself from him as I unfolded the mess of a letter. My hands started to shake as I read.

"No . . . oh God, no!" I fell to my knees, instantly feeling sick.

***

I stood between Lillian and Helen, holding their hands and staring blankly at Eric's coffin. How was he gone? He was in Africa . . . wasn't the war in Europe? And yet here we were, standing by his graveside, and it made no sense to me. When the priest finished speaking, people began to lay flowers on his coffin. When it was my turn, I numbly walked over and laid down the carnation I was holding. I then placed my hand on the smooth wooden box that held my brother. Tears continued pouring down my face, and I didn't bother to wipe them away—it would have done no good as they kept coming. *God why did you take him?* I thought to myself. *He was young and so full of life. Why didn't you take Frank instead? I wouldn't have cared . . . you would have been doing me a favor.* Eric's last letter to me had been dated just four days before the letter my papa received. I didn't understand what Eric had written to me, and now I even understood less. *How could you take him God? He loved you, and you killed him.* I wanted to shout at the top of my lungs. I was so angry. But somehow, I kept myself from doing so and just stood silently, looking at the coffin. Lillian grabbed hold of my arm, snapping me out of my thoughts. I looked over at her, and she, too, had tears running down her face. She gently pulled me away, and as she did, I glanced at Mama's grave. *Mama won't be alone now,* I thought to myself. And then it hit me . . . not only was Mama gone, but Eric was also gone . . . I was now truly alone. I was hurt and angry at God, and I decided right there and then that I did not need him . . . I did not want him. I did not want anything to do with a God who took my loved ones away.

***

A week later, I received another letter. This time it was about Frank. He wasn't dead . . . he was injured and would be returning home within the month. I sat at the kitchen table reading and rereading the letter. I didn't want Frank to return. Life this past year had been good without him. Yes, I was alone most the time, but I was happy. When Frank returned, things would just go back to how they used to be. I didn't want him to touch me, and I didn't want to be beaten anymore either. Standing from the table, I walked over to a cabinet and removed a coffee can. Opening the lid, I pulled out all the money. I quickly counted it. I didn't have a lot. Frank never sent home any of the money he earned from his service, so the only money I had was what I earned on the farm. And after I paid the boys their share for doing all the hard work, there wasn't much left. What little I did have I had been using to live on, but still, it was something. Removing my apron, I threw it over a chair, and with the money still in hand, I ran upstairs. Entering into one of the spare rooms, I opened the wardrobe. I had remembered seeing a bag stashed away. Moving a few items around, I found it. I grabbed the bag and took it into my room. Setting the bag on the bed, I opened my drawer and took out my three dresses. I had purchased material in town a couple years back and had made the dresses myself. When I turned sixteen, my body changed—my chest had grown and was full, and I had curves where I was once tall and lanky. I could no longer wear my childhood dresses . . . of course, they were so old and threadbare that even if I could still fit into them, they needed to be replaced long before they had been anyway. I placed my nightgown and undergarments into the bag as well as my brush and a few other items I would need. I retrieved my tin from under the mattress where I kept it hidden and placed it into the bag on top of everything else. The money—I was still holding tightly to it. I took a sock from Frank's drawer, placed the money inside, and put it, too, in the bag. I took a quick look around the room, making sure I had everything I needed. Then, picking up the bag, I went downstairs. Sitting on the bench by the front door, I slipped on my shoes. I had purchased them last year. They were the first new shoes I had ever owned, and they fit me perfectly. I did not wear them often, just when I went to town on occasion. In fact, the last time I wore them was the day of Eric's funeral. Once my shoes were on, I stood and grabbed my coat off the rack. As I put it on, I looked around. I would not miss this place that I had called home for the past several years.

I wondered if I should go over to Papa's and see if I could convince Lillian to join me. But I quickly realized I couldn't…if Papa found out I was leaving Frank, he would prevent me from doing so. Plus, my walk to town from here was already going to be a hike. Perhaps after I was settled somewhere, I could write to Lillian, but then I remembered she couldn't read. But I could write to Mary. Mary could get the letter to Lillian and read it to her as well. I could even send Lillian money for bus fare so she could join me . . . yes, that is what I would do. I hated to leave town without saying goodbye to Lillian, but I had no choice. Picking up my bag, I opened the door and stepped outside. No sooner than I did, a cold breeze blew . . . I was tired of the cold. Maybe I would go somewhere warm. I shut the front door behind me, and as my feet touched the last step,

I remembered I had one last thing to do before I could leave, so I set my bag down onto the porch and began walking toward the barn.

Another cold breeze blew past, and I wrapped my arms around myself, trying to keep warm. Finally, I arrived at my baby's grave. I looked up at the tree. It was bare, but I could see the tiny green buds where the new spring leaves would soon be blossoming. "I'm leaving . . . I came to say goodbye," I said as I knelt. Immediately, tears ran down my cheeks—they always did. "I love you . . . I will always love you." I kissed the tips of my fingers and touched the stone marker then stood and walked away. I wasn't sure what else to say, or if I should even bother to speak, because I didn't want to chicken out and stay.

Once back at the house, I grabbed my bag off the porch and started off down the drive. Frank's truck was here, but I had no idea how to drive, so I was walking to town. *Am I really doing this?* I thought as I stepped off our property onto the dirt lane. *Leaving my husband? Leaving this town? Leaving behind everything I know? Can I really do this?* I could, and I would, because if I stayed, I knew what my future was. Nearing the end of the lane, Mary's house came into view. I'd forgotten all about Mary. If she saw me, she would come out and start asking me questions. Should I wait and leave after dark? No, it wouldn't be safe or proper for a lady to walk the streets after dark. Perhaps she wouldn't see me. I continued on, looking down at the dirt road as I passed by her house.

"Anne!" I sighed. Mary was a sweet lady, but she was nosy. "Anne!" she called again. Closing my eyes, I took a deep breath and continued walking, pretending like I didn't hear her. "Anne, what are you up to?"

Out of the corner of my eye, I could see her running my direction. "Just taking a walk," I replied, looking her way and forcing a smile.

"Anne, wait up," she said, rushing over. She stepped in front of me, cutting me off. Holding her sweater closed, she looked me over. I stood quietly, holding my bag behind my back and trying my best to hide it. "Anne, what are you doing?" she asked. "Where are you going?" I shook my head. "Anne," she said, reaching out and touching my arm.

"I can't stay," I said as tears formed in my eyes. "There is nothing here for me."

"Oh, Anne," she said, hugging me. "I know you miss your brother Eric, but you're not alone."

"No, Mary, you don't understand . . . it's Frank. I received a letter today."

Mary's eyes went big as she placed her hand over her mouth. "Oh, honey, I'm sorry. But you don't have to leave just because Frank is dead."

"He's not dead," I whispered.

"I don't understand," she said, holding me at arm's length and looking at me, confused.

"He's injured, and they're sending him home. He'll arrive soon, probably any day now according to when the letter was dated. Mary, I . . . I can't do it anymore. He drinks a lot, and when he does, he beats me, and his touch . . . I . . . I . . . ."

Mary nodded. "Sweetie, how old are you?"

"Eighteen," I whispered.

She closed her eyes and sighed then opened them once again. "I knew you were young, but I didn't realize you were that young when he took you. And I should have known when the doctor found those bruises on you that it was Frank, that you hadn't fallen. I'm so sorry, Anne. Tell me where you're going. If you go to your papa's house, Frank will just fetch you back."

"I know . . . I'm not going home."

"Then where are you going?" I shrugged my shoulders. "Do have any money?"

"A little," I replied. "Enough for a bus ticket to somewhere."

"Are you sure you want to do this? A woman living on her own? What are you going to do for a job?"

"I have to do this, Mary . . . if I stay, I know my future. And besides, there are lots of women living alone nowadays, lots of jobs available too. I'm sure I can find something."

She nodded. "Who's going to take care of the animals until Frank returns?" she asked. The animals? I had left in such a hurry that I hadn't even thought about the animals. I sighed. I couldn't leave—I was stuck, I thought, but then Mary said, "I'll send my Henry over until Frank arrives home."

"Really?" I asked, surprised. "Will he have time? I know he's busy here helping you, and I can't pay him."

"Don't you worry about that, Anne. We're friends and neighbors. Isn't that what we're here for, to help each other?" I nodded, smiling slightly. Mary smiled back. "Now I wish I could give you some money, but I don't have any to spare. However, I have a truck, and I know how to drive. Let me drive you to town so you don't have to walk in this weather. It looks like it might rain."

***

"When you get settled somewhere, you write me," Mary said as we sat in her truck just out front of the bus depot. "Promise me you'll write. I want to know you're okay. And if things don't work out, you let me know, and we'll get you home."

"I promise I'll write," I replied. "Thank you for the ride and for everything, Mary. The truth is, I don't know how I would have survived all these years without your friendship."

She smiled, and I could tell she was holding back tears. "Good luck, Anne."

I nodded then opened the door. I stepped out and, quickly closing the door, I ran for cover. I was glad Mary had offered to give me a ride because she was right, it had begun to rain on our drive into town, and it was now pouring. Once under cover, I turned around. She waved as she drove off, and I waved back. When I could no longer see her truck, I entered the bus station. An older man was sitting in a chair nearest the door. His head was back, and his eyes were closed—most likely sleeping. Three young boys in uniform were waiting for a bus as well. They looked to be sixteen, maybe seventeen years old. They were all talking and laughing, having a good time. I wondered if they had any idea what they were about to experience. Would they return home alive or in a box like Eric? I took a deep breath and held in my tears at the thought of Eric. I hadn't said goodbye to him or Mama. I hadn't thought to ask Mary to take me by the graveyard. Of course, in this rain, it wouldn't have been a good idea. I would most likely get sick. I continued on toward the ticket booth and stood in line behind a young woman who had a small child in tow. The little girl turned around and looked up at me. "Hello," she whispered shyly, smiling.

"Hello," I replied, smiling back at her.

When the young woman finished purchasing her tickets, she turned around and grabbed the little girl's hand. "Come along, Grace."

She, too, smiled at me as she stepped to the side, and once again, I smiled back, then stepped up to the counter. A young woman who looked to be around my age stood behind the metal bars that separated us. If she could get a job, then surely I could. "May I help you?" she asked.

"Yes, I would like to purchase a ticket."

"To where?" she asked. *To where?* I had not even thought about where I was going other than the possibility of going somewhere warm. Warm meant south—I knew that much. Looking to my left, I saw a map of the United States posted on the wall showing the bus routes. Just south of Virginia was a state called North Carolina . . . I did not want to be north. Then there was South Carolina. But I thought perhaps it would be too close to Virginia. Georgia, Florida, Alabama . . . "Miss?" she said, getting my attention.

"Alabama," I said, though it sounded more like a question than a statement.

"Where in Alabama?" she then asked. *Where?* Once again, I had no idea. "Huntsville, Birmingham, Montgomery," she said, naming cities.

"Montgomery," I said, having no idea where this Montgomery, Alabama was exactly. "I want to go to Montgomery."

***

Opening my eyes, I was surprised I had been able to sleep sitting in this bus seat. I didn't know what time it was or where we were, but by the light, I guessed it was very early morning. I had to use the restroom and hoped the bus would be stopping somewhere soon. Looking around, I saw that most everyone was still asleep, though I could hear a few hushed conversations going on behind me several rows back.

"Did you sleep well?"

I turned my head to see Marley was awake as well. She was the young mother who had purchased her ticket just before I did. Her sister's husband had been killed in combat, and Marley was on her way down to Atlanta, Georgia to stay with her sister for a while. "Better than I expected," I replied. Her daughter Grace was sleeping on the seat beside her with her head resting on Marley's lap. "Do you know if the bus will be stopping soon?" I asked.

"I don't know, but I hope so. I need to use the restroom," she whispered. I smiled and nodded. "So, Anne, you never told me where you were going."

"Alabama," I said.

"What part?"

"Montgomery."

"The capital." I nodded though I'd had no idea that Montgomery was the capital of Alabama until just then. "You have family there?" she asked.

"Yes," I said, lying because I didn't want her to think of me a wild woman.

The bus slowed down, and I turned my head, looking out the window once again. I was pleased to see we were pulling into a rest stop.

***

Back on the bus, my stomach had begun to growl. In my rush to leave, I'd forgotten to pack any food. I hadn't eaten anything since breakfast yesterday morning, and now it was breakfast the following day. I still had a bit of money to purchase food, but there were no stores in which to do so at the rest stops. I would just have to wait and eat later. As the minutes passed, people all around began to pull out their food, Marley included. The smell of the food made my stomach turn even more.

"Now hold still," Marley said to Grace as she laid a cloth over the little girl's lap. I watched as she placed a boiled egg, a piece of bread, and a wedge of cheese on the cloth. I turned my head to look out the window, trying to keep my mind off my empty stomach. It wasn't the first time in my life I had felt hunger pains. When I was living with Papa, we had so many mouths to feed, and there wasn't always enough food to go around. Especially by late winter to early spring, when we would run out of canned goods, and the garden wasn't yet ready for harvest. Papa always ate, and I made sure the little kids always got something in their stomachs even if it wasn't much. It was Eric and me who would sacrifice. We took turns—if I missed a meal and he ate, then the next meal I got to eat, and he didn't. And on occasion, we both had gone without. "Aren't you going to eat, Anne?" Marley asked minutes later.

"No," I whispered as I shook my head.

"Do you have anything to eat?" she asked. I shook my head again. "Well, why didn't you say? I have plenty," she said as she opened her basket.

Retrieving a piece of bread, cheese, and an apple, she handed the items across the aisle to me. "Thank you," I said as I took the food. "In my excitement to leave, I forgot to pack food."

She smiled. "It's alright. I might have done the same if I didn't have Grace to look after."

FOUR

Marley and Grace got off the bus in Atlanta, and I still had a few hours' ride to my destination. It was strange . . . even though I hardly knew Marley, I missed her presence and her company. As the bus crossed the state line from Georgia into Alabama, I became more and more anxious. I really hadn't thought this out . . . I had no job, no family, nowhere to stay, and very little money. What was I going to do? Would anyone even hire me? I hardly had any education, and aside from caring for a house and children, I had never worked outside the home. Where would I live? Women didn't live alone. I mean, married women lived alone with their husbands gone due to the war, but single women didn't. I couldn't do this on my own . . . I hated to admit it, but I needed Frank. I needed him to take care of me. I began to panic, and I took several deep breaths to calm myself. When I arrived in Montgomery, I would go straight to the ticket booth and purchase a ticket back to Virginia. I would go home, and hopefully I would arrive before Frank did. He would have no idea I had left . . . no one aside from Mary would know I had been gone.

A few hours later, the bus entered a large city. It wasn't nearly as large as Atlanta was, nor were the buildings as tall, but still, the city of Montgomery was much larger than the little town I had grown up in. I looked out the window as we passed several neighborhoods, churches, and businesses. We then went past some large white buildings. One of them had a huge domed top. I had never seen anything like it before, and I wondered if it was a real palace. I was amazed, and I thought perhaps I could stay for just one day and have a look around before I returned home. I would have to count my money. I wasn't sure I had enough for meals, a hotel room, and bus fare, but if I did . . . I was going to stay and have a look around. Finally, the bus pulled into the station, and once it came to a full stop, I stood. Clutching my bag tight, I waited in line as people slowly filed off the bus. Once inside the depot, I looked around for the ladies' room. I wanted a private place to count my money so I could decide what I was going to do. Spotting the sign on the opposite side of the large waiting room, I began making my way toward the restroom. I had only gone a few steps when I felt a hand on my arm. It was an older woman who stopped me. She was slightly shorter than me, and her white hair was pulled up neatly. She wore a yellow hat that went well with her navy-blue dress, that had a yellow and red floral print. She had a frilly collar and her sleeves were trimmed in a fancy lace. Her brown shoes were polished, and she wore white gloves on her hands. She looked dressed and ready for church even though it was a Thursday. "Bethany?"

"No, ma'am, I'm sorry," I replied. "I'm not Bethany."

"Well, it was a good guess," she said, smiling. "What's your name then?"

I hesitated, wondering if I should tell a stranger my name . . . then again, she was an old lady, so what harm could it do? "Anne. My name is Anne."

"Well, Anne, it's nice to meet you. My name is Agatha, but you can call me Aggie . . . my friends call me Aggie, and we're friends, are we not?" I smiled and nodded my head, wondering where this lady's family was because she was obviously not all there. "Well, we should get going. Do you have all your things?"

"Going?" I asked, confused.

"Home, of course. Where else would we be going?"

"Home? Your home?"

Aggie smiled. "Once again, yes . . . do you think I would take you to someone else's house?" Shaking her head, she took hold of my arm, and we began walking toward the doors. I wanted to protest, but for some reason, I followed. "We could take the trolley, but it's such a nice day, and you've just spent many hours cooped up on a bus. A walk will do us both good."

"How far do you live from here?" I asked, still wondering why I was following this lady.

"About ten blocks, maybe twelve . . . not too far. So where are you from, Anne?"

"Virginia."

"Virginia . . . never been there. I've been to North Carolina, but that's as far north as I ever dared to venture."

Aggie talked and talked the entire eleven blocks to her home on St. Charles. I had never known anyone who talked as much as Aggie. "Well, here it is," she said excitedly as we stood in front of a small one-story house. It was tiny and looked more like a cottage. The house was blue with white trim, and it had a brick foundation. There were four potted ferns hanging from the front porch. Two wicker sofas and a couple of tables also adorned the porch. Colorful flowers were growing along the brick path that ran from the sidewalk to the front porch steps, and a white picket fence surrounded the house. Two medium-sized trees sat in the front yard, and I could tell their leaves had just recently bloomed as they were tiny and a brilliant green. Everything was very well-kept, and the house was quaint. "Come, come," she said, placing her hand on the small of my back and ushering me in through the gate. Still wondering what I was doing here, I slowly walked up the path and then the steps onto the porch, where I stood slightly off to the side as Aggie opened the bright red front door.

"Go on," she said, smiling, as she ushered me inside. The living room was small but very cute with a sofa, love seat, and a braided rug covering the wood floor. There were a couple of side tables, each lined with doilies, and one had an oil lamp sitting on top. But there was no need for the lamp because a light fixture hung from the ceiling in the center of the room, and there were two sconces on the wall on either side of the fireplace mantel—this house had electricity.

Sure, I had seen electric lights before when I went to town—all the businesses had them—and I knew some houses had them as well, but I had never lived in a house that was electrified. Even Mary's house was not electrified. I then noticed a piano with a radio sitting on top.

Aggie walked past me, and I followed her through a set of French doors into a formal dining room. There was a table with six chairs in the center of the room sitting atop another braided rug. A china cabinet rested against the far wall, and it was filled with fancy china. I walked over and looked through the glass. I had never seen anything so beautiful or delicate before. And I couldn't imagine eating off dishes so nice. This room, too, had a fireplace, and a picture of a man was hung over the mantel. "My late husband George," Aggie said, looking up at the picture. I could see the love and adoration she had for him in her eyes, and I knew George was nothing like Frank. "We were married for over sixty years. He built this house for me in 1920," she continued. "Purchased it out of a Sears catalog. It's not big, but we didn't need a big house as we never did have any children."

I smiled then looked around the room once again. Seeing a switch on the wall beside me, I pushed the button, causing the lights in the chandelier that hung over the dining room table to flicker on. I pushed it again, and the lights went off. I pushed it yet again, turning it back on. "Sorry," I said when I noticed Aggie was watching me. "I ain't never had electric lights."

"You *have never* had electric lights," she said, correcting my speech. "Now this way, dear," she said as she motioned me toward a hall just off the dining room. I followed her into the small hall, and she opened a door on the right. "This will be your room, Anne."

I stepped inside and was amazed. The room looked like it was out of a magazine. The walls were papered with a pink rose and striped print. A white metal bed, dressed in a bright white lacy bedspread, was positioned on the wall to my left between two large windows. A quilt rack with two quilts stood at the end of the bed.

Two small nightstands flanked each side of the bed, each with matching lamps. A wardrobe stood on the other wall between two more windows. All the windows were adorned with fancy white lace curtains that matched the bedding. On the wall opposite the foot of the bed was a fireplace with a brick mantel. Seeing a small door beside the fireplace, I walked over and opened it . . . it was a closet. I had never had a closet before. Closing the closet door, I looked in Aggie's direction and saw there was a vanity with a large mirror on the wall just beside the door where she was standing and watching me. "This is all mine?" I asked, shocked.

"Yes . . . do you like it?"

"I do," I replied, looking around and still not believing this was happening to me. "I've never had such a nice room before."

"Well, I'm glad you like it. Just one week ago, this was my husband's study." With tears welling up in her eyes, she reached out and ran her fingers over the smooth top of the vanity. "But I think this serves a much better purpose now." I set my bag at the foot of the bed, not knowing what to say. I could see the pain and the hurt in her eyes. I imagined it was a lot stronger than the pain and hurt I felt for Eric because she had had many more years with George than I ever had with Eric. "The washroom is this way," she said as she left the room. I followed her back into the hall just as she opened another door. It was a real washroom inside a house. I mean, I knew people had them . . . but not where I lived . . . at least not the farmhouses I had been in. We still used outhouses and washbasins and bathed in the kitchen in our metal tubs. Blue and yellow tiles adorned the floor and the walls. There was a sink, a commode, and a bathtub . . . all porcelain. It was beautiful, if washrooms could ever be considered beautiful. "Well, I'm sure you would like to get settled in and clean up. I'm going to start dinner. You will find towels and everything else you might need in the closet," she said, pointing to the linen closet in the washroom. "Take your time, Anne, and join me in the kitchen when you're done."

***

The bath was amazing . . . I was amazed that I could choose hot or cold water, and within minutes, the tub was filled. I sat and soaked until the water turned cold, and I was forced to get out. Then, when I pulled the plug to the drain, I watched until every last drop was gone, wondering the entire time where all the water came from and where it went. After I had dried off, I noticed a robe hanging on the hook behind the door. It was pale pink with a decorative white trim and three small roses embroidered in the corner of the collar. I realized I had no robe—I had never needed one before. Taking the robe off the hook, I hoped Aggie wouldn't mind me borrowing it. Leaving the washroom, I went to my room . . . *my* room. It seemed so strange. It was like a fairy tale. I'd never had a room all to myself before. Well, I guess I did when Frank was gone, but still, I never thought of it as my room. And I never imagined I would ever be sleeping in a room as nice as this was. It was strange how just this morning I was worried about where I was going to go and what I was going to do, and out of nowhere, Aggie appeared. I walked over to the windows that faced the front of the house. I had a view of the street and the others houses across it. I closed the blinds then walked over to the other set of windows and closed the blinds on them as well. All I could see out of those windows was the side of the neighbor's house. And the house was close—only about five feet separated the two. I wasn't used to living in such close proximity to others, having to close windows for privacy. Living in the country, we always left our windows open. There was no need to close them as no one was ever around. With the windows shut, I opened my bag and removed all my belongings. I placed my undergarments and nightgown in the wardrobe, then hung my dresses in the closet with the exception of my red dress with its tiny white dots. That was the dress I was going to wear. It had a collar around the neckline and buttoned down the front with four white buttons then tied around my waist with a bow in the back. It was the nicest dress I owned, and after seeing what Aggie was wearing, I wanted to look nice. Once I was dressed, I looked in the mirror. My dress was wrinkled. I didn't have time to iron it, so I just pressed out the wrinkles with my hands as best as I could. I then combed through my hair and quickly pinned up the sides. I tried to smooth out my dress once more before I left the room. Walking through the dining room, I could smell the food. Seconds later, I stepped into a tiny kitchen. It was clean and tidy, just like everything else in the house, but it was tiny. There was no way my entire family would be able to take a meal in here. We just wouldn't fit. There was a small table with two chairs sitting under a large window that looked out into the backyard. The backyard itself was long and skinny. There were a few trees, and I could see places where there had once been flower beds. A clothesline and a small shed also sat in the backyard. On all sides, I could see more houses. Once again, seeing so many homes was strange to me. Two place settings sat on the table, and I was glad to see it was not set with the fancy dishes because I would have been afraid to eat off those. A basket of bread and a bowl of green beans had already been set out.

"Please sit," Aggie said, motioning to the table. "I hope you like spaghetti."

"I've never had spaghetti," I said as I sat.

"Never had spaghetti?"

"No, ma'am. I grew up on a farm . . . we ate what we grew."

"Well then, you will be in for a treat night after night," she said as she set a bowl of what I assumed to be spaghetti down onto the table between the green beans and the basket of bread. It looked like a basket full of yarn with some kind of red sauce poured over the top. "My friends and I swap recipes. I like to try new foods." Once Aggie sat, I reached into the bread basket. "No," she said, slapping my hand. "Not until we say grace."

"Sorry," I whispered as I pulled my hand back and placed it in my lap.

I remembered saying grace before meals when I was a small child. After Mama died, we no longer did. I didn't want to talk to God, but I wasn't going to argue with Aggie, so I bowed my head and pretended to pray. When Aggie had finished saying grace, she plopped a large scoop of spaghetti onto my plate. "Try it," she said. I picked up my fork but wasn't quite sure how to eat it. "Like this," she said, showing me how to twirl the noodles onto my fork. I followed her instructions and took a bite. "So what do you think?" she asked.

"It's delicious," I replied after I had swallowed. "Really good."

"Have you ever eaten a cheeseburger and fries before?" she asked. I shook my head. "I didn't think so. Tomorrow, for lunch, I'm going to take you downtown. I know a place that serves the best cheeseburgers. We can even order milkshakes. So if you think this meal is good . . . just wait until tomorrow."

***

"That was delicious," I said, stuffed when the meal was over.

"I'm glad you enjoyed it," Aggie replied. "And I was glad for the company."

I smiled then looked back out the window. The sun had gone down while we ate dinner, and now I could see streetlights shining from a distance as well as lights from the surrounding homes.

"You like being outdoors, don't you?"

"Yes," I replied, turning to look at Aggie.

"My George did too," she said. "He would plant flowers each spring, and by summer our yard was beautiful. I don't have a green thumb, but I sure enjoyed his flowers. I'll miss the flowers. This will be the first year I don't have a garden."

"I could plant flowers if you'd like," I said. "I know how to tend a garden, and I enjoy it."

Aggie smiled. "I would like that."

***

The next morning, I found Aggie sitting in the living room reading a book. As I neared, I realized it was a Bible she was reading. I looked at the clock, surprised to see how late it was . . . I had slept right through breakfast, and I had only done so one other time in my life.

"Did you sleep well?" Aggie asked, looking up.

"Yes, I did, and I apologize for sleeping so late."

"Oh, no worries, dear," she said, waving her hand. "You were tired after your travels. So I was thinking after lunch today we could go to the store and buy you a few new dresses."

"Store-bought dresses?" I asked, surprised.

"Of course."

"Aggie, I appreciate all you've done for me, but can I ask you why?" I said as I sat on the sofa beside her. "I mean, you don't even know me."

Aggie smiled, and then reaching out, she took my hand. "You are correct—I don't know you . . . but I will get to."

"I still don't understand."

"God knows you, dear, and he knows your needs. He's the one who told me to go to the bus station and look for a young woman who needed a family."

"How did you know it was me?" I asked in a whisper, now thinking this woman was completely crazy.

"Because you looked lost and frightened."

FIVE

March 1944

A year had passed since I had moved in with Aggie. It still seemed like a fairy tale at times. Aggie treated me as if I were her daughter. Like she had said, she and her late husband never did have any children, so perhaps I filled that void. Regardless, my life had drastically changed. Aggie taught me how to be a refined woman—she taught me how to speak properly, how to be a good hostess and entertain my guests, how to play the piano, and how to cook dishes I had never even heard of before. She even introduced me to a whole new world through books. We went weekly to the library, and when I was not busy helping around the house or tending the flower garden in the backyard, my nose was in a book. I could now read and write proficiently. Then there was church. Church was a huge part of Aggie's life. We went every Sunday and Wednesday. We never missed. Aggie was in the choir and played the piano on occasion when the pastor's wife wasn't able. She was involved with almost all the church functions. I went because I had no choice—this was Aggie's life, and I was blessed to be a part of it. I played along, but inside, I hated God . . . I was still angry. Life was full of one activity after another. My new 'friends' were all older women, mostly widowed, and all around Aggie's age.

Thinking back, I never did have any friends my own age. Even Mary was several years older than me. I wrote to her a few days after I had first arrived in Montgomery, letting her know I was okay. We kept in touch, writing once a month, and she kept me updated on my family. Last she heard, Jeremy was still fighting overseas, and he was alive and well. Her own husband had been injured. He'd lost his left arm, so he was now back home. Unfortunately, her eldest son Henry, now of age, was gone, shipped off overseas. Frank, of course, was back and had been for a year now. He arrived home just a week after I left, and Mary told me he was not at all happy when he discovered I was missing. Of course, she pretended like she knew nothing of my whereabouts. Told him she came to visit, and I was gone, so she sent her son to take care of the animals until he returned. Unlike her husband, Frank had all his limbs . . . it was his face that was the problem. He had been caught in a fire and was blind in one eye. She told me that Papa still drank . . . now worse than ever before. The death of Eric had hit him hard, and I prayed for his sake that Jeremy would live. Mary said Papa stayed so drunk all the time that the twins, now in their teens, were running Papa's farm. She told me that Lillian and Helen were doing well, and that little Mike, not so little anymore at ten, was growing like a weed. I missed my family more than I thought I would. Still, I knew I was much better off living here with Aggie than I would be back home. I never did send for Lillian like I had planned. If I had been working and supporting myself, I definitely would have, but since Aggie was taking care of me and paying for everything, I never asked. To burden her with the care of yet another person, well, it just didn't seem right. I folded the letter from Mary and placed it in my book. Closing the book, I looked up from where I was sitting on the porch and was surprised to see a man in uniform standing on the porch by the front door, watching me. "Letter from a love overseas?" he asked.

He was very handsome. Tall and slender but not too skinny. Blonde hair, green eyes . . . and he smiled, exposing his dimples. He was older than me, looked to be about thirty or so. "No," I replied shyly. "From a girlfriend."

"No man overseas?" he asked as he dropped his cigarette to the ground then stepped on it.

"No," I replied, now blushing. "Other than my younger brother . . . no."

Just then, the screen door opened, and Aggie stepped out onto the porch carrying a tray of sweet tea. "Heavens!" she exclaimed. "Is it really you, Samuel?" She quickly set the tray down, and then the two embraced. I stood from my chair and watched, wondering who this man was to Aggie as I knew she had no children. "Are you back for good," she asked, holding him at arm's length and looking him over.

"I am," he replied.

"Is the war over?" she asked with hopefulness in her voice. "Please sit," she then said before he had a chance to answer.

As he walked to the nearest chair, I noticed he had a slight limp. As he sat, I too sat back down. "No, the war isn't over, not yet," he explained as he removed his hat and set it on his knee. "I was shot."

"Shot! You were shot, and I'm just now hearing about this?" Aggie said, voice raised.

He smiled and took Aggie's hand in his. "It wasn't fatal, and I knew it . . . so I told them not to inform you." Aggie relaxed a bit, and then Samuel turned his attention to me. "So who is this stunning beauty?"

Once again, I could feel myself turning red. "Anne," Aggie said. "This is Anne . . . she's living with me now."

"Good," he replied. "I'm glad to hear you're not alone, Aunt Aggie." Aunt . . . now I knew the relation. Was it from her side or her husband's? I still did not know. "Sam," he said, holding his hand out to me.

"It's a pleasure to meet you, Sam," I said, taking his hand.

"Pleasure is all mine," he replied, smiling and exposing those dimples once again.

Again, I felt myself blushing. Why was I so attracted to this man? I smiled shyly as I pulled my hand away.

"Have you been home yet?" Aggie asked.

"No, I came here to see you first."

"Sam lives in Birmingham," she explained. "He's a traveling salesman . . . very good at what he does."

"*Was* a salesman, Aunt Aggie," he said, pouring a glass of tea. "I don't know if they will give me my job back." He offered me the glass.

"Thank you," I replied, taking it.

"So, Anne, where are you from?" he asked as he poured another glass of tea.

"Virginia."

"Where about?" he asked after he took a sip of his drink.

"It was a small farming community . . . you won't have heard of it. Nothing fascinating ever happens there."

"Oh, I don't know if that's true. You fascinate me."

I looked down, once again blushing.

"Do behave yourself Samuel, or I'll have to ask you to leave," Aggie said.

Samuel chuckled, but I couldn't tell if Aggie was joking or not. "The tea was delicious, Aunt Aggie," he said, setting his glass down and standing.

"Are you leaving so soon?" she asked, standing.

"Not for a few days," he said.

"Where are you staying?"

"I don't know . . . I was hoping to stay here, but that was before I realized you had company. I'll get a hotel room downtown."

"Do you need any money?"

"No," he replied as he put on his hat. "I have plenty of money. I was just hoping to spend some time with you."

"Will you join us for dinner then?" Aggie asked.

"Tonight?"

"Yes, tonight," she replied, "and every night you're here in town."

"I would be glad to join you," he said. "Except for Friday. I might have plans."

"What plans do you have on Friday that would keep you away?" Aggie asked curiously.

Sam looked at me. "Well, I was hoping I could convince a certain young woman to allow me to take her to dinner and perhaps a movie."

"Me? You want to take me out?" I asked, standing to my feet. Sam smiled as he nodded. I had never been asked out before . . . I had never even been out on a date. I looked at Aggie, not sure how I should answer. She just smiled and nodded. "Yes," I whispered.

"Well, it looks like I have plans Friday, Aunt Aggie," he said, placing his hat back on his head. "But I will be here otherwise. See you ladies later."

I watched as Sam walked down the steps, down the path, out the gate, and down the sidewalk. I could feel my heart pounding in my chest. Was I really going on a date . . . and to the movies? I had never been to a movie. When I turned around, Aggie was smiling.

"I remember my first date with George," she said. "He took me on a picnic after church one Sunday. It rained, and all the food he prepared—or should I say that his sisters prepared—was ruined." She smiled. "He told me he had made the food, but I came to find out years later that his sisters had made it for him. I should have known . . . because he had no cooking skills whatsoever! So shall we go inside and decide what you're going to wear on your first date?"

"Friday is two days away," I replied.

"Yes, which means if we can't find anything suitable, then we will have time to buy something."

***

I stood nervously looking at myself in the full-length mirror Aggie had in her bedroom. She insisted that we purchase a new dress for my date. I tried to argue—I had several nice dresses I could wear, and I didn't want her to spend the money—but she insisted, said it was a special occasion, and told me I could wear my new dress for Easter as well. We had gone to the department store yesterday, and I chose a pale yellow dress with yellow lace trim. It was really pretty against my dark hair and blue eyes. And even I had to admit that the style really flattered my figure.

"Here," Aggie said, handing me a red lipstick. "Put a little of this on." She had already done my hair, setting it in curlers earlier in the day, and put a bit of blush on my cheeks as well. I put the lipstick on and then handed it back. "Look at you . . . you are the prettiest woman I have seen in a long time. No wonder my nephew is smitten with you."

"Or perhaps he has been overseas so long that the company of any woman is comforting," I said.

"Don't sell yourself short, Anne. You are an amazing and beautiful woman. Any man would be lucky to have you as his wife." I forced a smile. That was the thing. I had been a man's wife, and I never wanted to be a wife again. But Aggie didn't know that. She never asked me about my past, so I never said anything. "I bet that's Sam," she said as we heard a knock on the front door. "Come out when you're ready."

I nodded and watched as she left the room. Seconds later, I could hear their voices in the living room—it was Sam. Suddenly I was nervous. What was I doing going out with Sam? I didn't want to get married. It was just a date, I told myself. I was being silly. We weren't getting married. We had just met. Still, should I even be going out? After all, I was married. I looked down at my left hand. I never had a wedding ring, never had a wedding. Sometimes I wondered if Frank and I were really married. I hoped so . . . though I hated him. The thought of living as man and wife and not really being married . . . looking at myself in the mirror once again, I took a deep breath. Married or not, I was not with Frank anymore. As I entered the living room, Sam stopped speaking to Aggie and just stared at me.

"Wow, you look amazing," he said seconds later, just above a whisper. Once again, I blushed. "Shall we?" he asked, offering me his arm.

"Don't forget your cardigan," Aggie said, rushing over to the hook by the door.

She removed my cardigan, and before I could take it from her, Sam did, and he held it open for me. I turned around, putting my right arm in first and then my left. He then took my hair and lifted it out from between my dress and the cardigan. When he did, his finger gently brushed up against my neck, and my heart leaped at his touch. Why was I having these strange feelings? I had never felt this way around a man before. "I won't have her out late, Aunt Aggie," Sam said, kissing her on the cheek as I turned around.

"I know you won't. Have fun you two," Aggie replied as she ushered us out the front door.

***

Sam took me to a really nice restaurant for dinner. It was fancy, and I felt out of place the entire time. I was glad Aggie taught me how to place my napkin on my lap and what all the silverware was for and when to use it. Still, I wasn't comfortable. I was afraid I might mess up. The choices on the menu were almost overwhelming. There were dishes I had never heard of before, and everything looked wonderful. And the prices were steep—I was surprised that anyone could afford to spend so much money on a meal. I ordered the cheapest meal I could find, chicken and rice . . . and it was good. Really good, much better than I had ever tasted before. Sam ordered a steak dinner, and his looked really good too. After dinner, we went to see a movie, and now Sam was walking me home. I was still not sure that I even liked the movie itself . . . but the experience of seeing a moving picture was fascinating. Sam had even got us popcorn to share.

"Want one?" Sam asked as he pulled a pack of cigarettes out of his coat pocket.

"No thank you. I don't smoke," I replied.

"Aggie rubbing off on you?"

Most people I knew smoked. It was common, but I had never picked it up. "No, I . . . just never felt the need."

He smiled. "How old are you, Anne?" he asked.

"Nineteen, and you?"

"Twenty-nine." I nodded. I had been close to guessing his correct age. "So tell me what brought you here, Anne. You have no family here, and from what my aunt has told me, she knows nothing of your past." I didn't answer right away . . . I wasn't sure what to say. What would Aggie think if she knew I had run away from my husband? What if she sent me back? "So what is your secret, Anne?" he asked. "Are you running from the law?" I stopped walking and looked at Sam seriously, then quickly realized he was joking as he had a smile on his face. "My, my, you're serious," he said.

"My brother was killed . . . "

"In the war?" he asked. I nodded. "I'm sorry."

"We were close. After he died, I realized there was nothing left for me back home . . . I was tired of the abuse and—"

"You were abused?"

I nodded. "Yes, and I couldn't take it anymore . . . the only way out was to leave. So with enough money for bus fare, I did just that."

"So you really came here not knowing what was going to happen to you?" he asked. I nodded my response then continued walking.

We walked silently the rest of the way home, and I wasn't sure what Sam was thinking. Perhaps I shouldn't have told him . . . perhaps I should have lied. We came to the house, and as I reached out for the gate, Sam took my hand.

"I'm glad you are here with Aunt Aggie."

"Me too," I said as he placed his other hand on my cheek.

The next thing I knew, his lips were touching mine. Once again, my heart was racing. Nervously, I stepped back. "Sam," I whispered.

"I'm sorry," he whispered back. "It's just . . . well, I find myself so attracted to you."

I knew exactly how he felt. I, too, realized just how attracted I was to him. "Well, goodnight then," I said, nervously trying to unlatch the gate and failing to do so.

"Let me," he said, placing his hand atop mine once again.

I looked at him, and our eyes locked. My heart began to race, and it scared me. These feelings I had for him scared me. As I pulled my hand away, he unlatched the gate then held it open for me. I quickly walked past, and about halfway up the path, I turned around to find he was still watching me. "Thank you for tonight," I said shyly. "I had fun."

He smiled. "I did too." I turned around and took a few more steps toward the house. "Anne," he called after me. I turned back around. "I'm leaving for Birmingham in the morning, but I was wondering if I could take you out again the next time I'm in town?"

"Yes, I would like that," I replied, smiling.

***

December 1945

Twenty-one months had passed since Sam and I first met. When he went back to Birmingham the first time, he managed to get his old job back, whichmeant he was often away, traveling. Sometimes for several months at a time. However, anytime he was in the area, he would come by to visit Aggie and, of course, take me out on a date. Life went on as normal for Aggie and me, church and all the other activities that went with it.

The best news was that the war had finally ended, so we had much to celebrate this Christmas. The last letter I received from Mary informed me that both Jeremy and her son were on their way home. I also had received a letter from Jeremy himself telling me the same. It was bittersweet. I was so very glad that both were alive, but I still missed Eric, and I was still so very angry at God that he, too, was not coming home. Almost every home had a blue star or stars hanging in the window, and it was not uncommon to see gold stars. Families missing loved ones. Just like Eric, there were so many men who had left never to return.

Aggie and I were knitting scarves for underprivileged children while listening to her nightly radio program. It was strange being on the giving end. Growing up, we were always one of the families that the church donated to.

"Who could it be this late?" Aggie asked as we heard a knock on the door.

I looked over at the clock that sat on the mantel. It was almost eight. The knock came again.

"I'll get it," I said, standing as I laid my knitting aside. Walking over to the door, I pushed the curtain aside and smiled. "It's Sam, Aggie," I said as I opened the door.

Sam stepped inside, removing his hat as he did. "We weren't expecting you," Aggie said, standing from the loveseat.

Sam kissed my cheek. "I wanted to surprise you," he said to Aggie as he removed his coat.

"That you did. Will you stay a bit? We have pumpkin pie."

"For your pie, Aunt Aggie, yes, I can stay," he replied as he hung his jacket on the hook by the door.

"Well, it's not my pie. Anne made it."

"Well, then I best be going," he teased. I playfully slapped Sam's arm as Aggie chuckled making her way towards the kitchen. "So I see she has you busy doing her good deeds," he said, looking over at the box of finished scarves sitting by the sofa.

"Yes, but I don't mind. It was by the good deeds of others that my family got by."

"You have a good heart," he said, smiling. "I like that about you."

Suddenly a crashing sound came from the kitchen. "Are you Alright Aggie?" I called out as I started towards the kitchen. When she didn't answer, I walked a bit faster. Upon entering the kitchen, I froze. Aggie was lying on the floor with broken plate pieces scattered all around. Pushing past me, Sam rushed to her side. "I'll call for help," I said, starting toward the phone.

"Anne," he said. I turned around. "I'm sorry," he said, shaking his head. "It's too late . . . she's gone."

***

Once again, I found myself standing by the grave of someone I loved. Aggie was gone, though it still seemed hard to believe. Back at the house during the wake, I half expected her to show up. It would be like Aggie to fake her own death. But it wasn't a joke. It was real, and she was gone. Members of her church and community had been over to the house all afternoon to give their condolences. Now everyone was gone, and it was quiet . . . too quiet. I turned on the radio while I cleaned up all the pies and casseroles that people had brought. I never understood why it was tradition to bring food when someone died. I was never hungry . . . I was always too sad to eat. Once the food was all put away, I walked into the living room and turned the radio off. I then looked around the house. I was alone. I didn't mind being alone when Frank had left for the war, but now . . . though Aggie was a tiny woman, her presence was large, and the house felt so empty. I wondered if I would even be able to sleep tonight. Sam had offered to stay, but I had told him no. Even though he would have stayed in Aggie's room, it was just not proper. Now, standing in this quiet house all alone, I wished I had agreed to let him stay. I turned off the light in the living room, and then just before I turned off the light in the dining room, I paused, looking at the picture of George. Was heaven real? And if so, was Aggie there, reunited with her beloved George? Was Eric there . . . Mama? I stood in place looking at the picture for several minutes, then I turned off the light and went to my room.

***

When I came into the living room the next morning, I was surprised to see Sam sitting on one of the sofas. I was glad I was fully dressed and hadn't come out in my nightgown thinking I was alone. "I let myself in," he said. I nodded. "Did you sleep alright last night?"

"As best as I could under the circumstances," I replied. He nodded then pulled out his cigarettes. Before I realized what he was doing, he lit one up. "Sam you need to put that cigarette out or take it outside. Aggie would never have allowed you to smoke in her house."

"She's not here, Anne," he argued.

"Sam," I said, voice raised. "I am not in the mood!"

"Alright," he said, putting the cigarette out.

"I'm sorry. I shouldn't have snapped at you."

"It's okay, Anne," he said as he approached. He placed his hands on my shoulders. "I miss her too." I nodded. "I'm meeting with a lawyer this morning," he said. "That's why I am here so early. You can stay if you wish."

"No, I think I'll go to the library. I really don't want to be here right now. It just doesn't feel right with Aggie gone."

He nodded. "I understand."

I stepped back, forcing Sam to release me, then walked over to the door where I put on my jacket. I then gathered up my books. "I'm sorry, Sam," I said, turning around to face him. "I should have offered you coffee or something."

"I'm fine," he replied. "You go on. If I want something, I know where to find it." I nodded again. "Smile, Anne," he said, smiling at me. "We're going to get through this."

I smiled. I didn't feel like smiling, but Sam with his dimples . . . well, I just couldn't help it. "Alright then, I will see you later," I said as I opened the front door.

Just then, a man came walking up the steps. He was older, perhaps mid-sixties, with gray hair and spectacles. His coat wasn't closed, and I could see he was wearing a fancy suit underneath. He was also carrying a briefcase, so I assumed he was the lawyer Sam was meeting with. "Morning," the man said when he saw me standing in the doorway.

"Good morning," I replied.

"I'm Mr. Lands, Aggie's lawyer. I'm here to meet with a Samuel Mathis."

"He's here. Please come in," I said, stepping back.

"And you are?" he asked as he stepped inside and removed his hat.

"Anne."

"Are you planning on going somewhere, Anne?" he asked as he looked me over.

"Yes, I was," I replied.

"I need you to stay if you don't mind."

"Okay," I said, closing the door and wondering why he wanted me here. I set my books down and removed my coat.

***

"Thank you," Mr. Lands said as I handed him a cup of coffee.

"You're welcome," I replied, handing one to Sam as well.

I sat on the sofa beside Sam across from where Mr. Lands was sitting on the loveseat.

"So I guess we should get started," Mr. Lands said, opening his briefcase and pulling out a file. "Mrs. Mathis wanted me to give you this letter after she passed." He pulled a paper from the file and handed it to Sam. "This one is for you," he said, holding out another to me.

I took the letter and slowly unfolded it. It was Aggie's familiar script.

> *My sweet Anne,*
>
> *If you are reading this letter, it means I have gone home to be with the Lord. Don't be sad for I am in a much better place and reunited with my beloved George.*

I looked up with tears already falling down my face. Mr. Lands and Sam sat quietly watching. I looked back down and continued to read.

You probably assumed that the day I found you at the bus depot I was blessing you, and I don't doubt that I was a blessing to you by any means. However, what I never told you was that my George had passed just a week earlier, and I was awfully lonesome, especially with Samuel my only living family member overseas. (And you know as well as I do that many of our young men who left never returned.) It was you, Anne, who blessed me. You will never know how much your company meant to a lonely old woman. You gave me a purpose, a reason to go on living. You are the daughter I never had, and I am so very blessed to have had you in my life. I know you are probably still wondering why I never asked you about your past. Well, there is an easy explanation. Your past doesn't matter. Remember that Jesus died for our sins, and if you trust in him, they are washed clean, cast away as far as the east is from the west. Don't look back, Anne. Keep moving forward. I'm tired, and I am ready to go home. The only reason I was holding on was because you needed a family. You don't need me anymore, Anne. My Sam was one of the lucky ones who came home . . . and he loves you. I don't know if he has told you that or not, but I can tell. You no longer need me—you have Sam. I can't tell the two of you what to do, but I do hope that the two of you will wed. Nothing would bring me more joy than to know that you are husband and wife. However, that being said, I don't want you to marry Sam just so you will have someone to care for you. So regardless of what choice you make, I want you to know that I left everything to you, Anne—the house, the money, all the investments. It isn't much, and you aren't rich, but if you are careful, you should be set for life. I don't ever want you to be without a home again. I love you, Anne. You are a sweet, beautiful, and strong woman. Most of all, I want you to know that God loves you. Follow him, Anne, and he will direct your every step.

Love Always, Aggie

Wiping my tears away, I looked up. "When did Aggie give this letter to you?"

"About two weeks ago," Mr. Lands replied.

"Did you read it?"

"Yes," he replied.

"Did she really leave me everything?" I asked, shocked.

"Yes."

"May I?" Sam asked, reaching out.

I handed him my letter and watched as he read. When he finished, he locked eyes with me for a moment, and I wondered what he was thinking. Aggie left everything to me, and he was her closest kin. Was he mad? He didn't look mad. Still . . .

"Anne, I just need you to sign a few documents, and then we will be done," Mr. Lands said seconds later, getting my attention.

***

I sat on the front porch with a blanket wrapped around me while Sam and Mr. Lands were inside speaking. It was cold, but I didn't want to be in the house. Aggie's presence was everywhere. She may have given me the house, but it wasn't my house, it was hers, and I missed her. "Why, why, God, did you take another loved one from me?" I whispered.

I could not understand how Aggie and Eric could love this God . . . this God that allowed bad things to happen to good people. Hearing the door open, I looked over as Mr. Lands stepped out, followed by Sam. "Good day, Anne," Mr. Lands said as he left.

I nodded and watched as he made his way down the steps, through the yard, and then over to his car that was parked in the street.

"You're going to freeze out here," Sam said as he walked over and sat in the chair beside mine.

"I can't go in . . . I miss her."

Reaching out, he took my hand in his. "So do I."

"Are you upset that she left everything to me?" I asked.

"No. I was surprised, but I don't need her money, and Aggie knew that. Plus, she didn't leave me totally empty-handed. She was right . . . I do love you." He then pulled a ring out of his pocket . . . it was Aggie's ring. "This is what she left me," he said, smiling. "Marry me, Anne. I know this isn't the most romantic proposal, and if you don't want this ring, then I will buy you another, but Anne, please say yes."

I wanted to . . . I wanted to say yes for I loved him too. I had for a long while now. But I couldn't. I was already married, so I couldn't marry Sam. "Sam . . . I . . . I can't."

"Is it the ring ? I already told you I would buy you another."

"It's not the ring, Sam," I whispered.

He shook his head as reached out, caressing my cheek. "I don't understand. Do you not love me?"

"That's not it," I said as tears once again fell from my eyes. "I do love you . . . but I can't marry you, Sam."

"Why not?" he asked as he removed his hand from my face. "Explain to me why, if you love me, you cannot marry me?"

"Because I am already wed to another."

Instantly, his face showed surprise. "You're only twenty. What do you mean you're married?" he said. "How old were you when you were married?"

"Fourteen," I whispered.

"But that's impossible. It's illegal."

"My papa owed a large debt," I began. "After my mother died, he began to drink. He had always drunk, but now he did so heavily, and he gambled too. He often owed money to others. When I was fourteen, he owed so much money that he was going to lose the house. A friend of his from whom he often borrowed money offered to pay his debt in exchange for me." I paused, wiping a tear away as the memories of that day came flooding back.

"How old was this man?" he asked.

"Frank . . . he was twenty-eight at the time."

Sam shook his head. "Did he . . . did he touch you in that way?" he asked.

I nodded as even more tears came pouring down my face.

"Oh, Anne, I'm so sorry," he said as he immediately took my hands in his.

"After we had been married for a couple months, I conceived," I continued. "I was so young and naïve that I didn't know how it happened, and I lost my baby that winter. I don't know if it was a boy or a girl—it was too early to tell. The doctor told me I lost the baby because I was so young, but I don't know if that's true or not. I never conceived again, and for all I know, I cannot have any more children. I was sixteen when the war began. My brother Eric and my husband Frank both left early on. I was glad Frank was gone. He, too, drank, and unlike my papa, who withdrew when he did so, Frank got violent, and he beat me often."

"I thought it was your father you had run from," Sam whispered.

I shook my head. "No, it was Frank. A week after we buried my brother Eric, I received a letter that Frank had been injured and was being sent home. While he was away, I lived free from his touch and the beatings . . . I couldn't go back to that life, so I took the little money I had saved, and I left. I came here on a whim, and Aggie found me. So you see, Sam, despite my feelings for you, I can't marry you, not when I belong to another. And I'm sorry, I'm so sorry I didn't tell you the truth sooner. I could have saved us both heartache."

Sam placed his hands on my face and, pulling me close, he kissed me. It was a long, deep, passionate kiss that sent sensations I had never felt before throughout my body. "You have nothing to be sorry about," he said minutes later. "You were a child when your father gave you to Frank. What he did was not only wrong, but it wasn't legal. And the fact that Frank . . . that he . . . what he did to you, it's disgusting, and it was wrong. And I'm so sorry, Anne, that he hurt you. But you see, you and Frank weren't married, which means you're free to marry me if you choose to do so. I love you, Anne, and if you say yes, I promise to love you until my last breath . . . and I will never hurt you. I will always cherish you. So what do you say?"

"Yes," I said, smiling through my tears. "I would love to marry you, Sam."

SIX

March 1946

Three days later, Sam and I married on Christmas Eve. Sam said he didn't want to wait to be married, and since it was so close to Christmas, we didn't have a large church wedding, nor did I get to wear a white dress. Instead, I wore the yellow dress that Aggie had bought me for our first date, and Sam had a friend of his who was certified marry us in the living room of Aggie's house. Legally, the house was mine, but I would always think of it as Aggie's home. It was just the three of us. We did not invite any friends or family, not that I had any to invite. After the ceremony, Sam and I went for dinner at the fancy restaurant downtown that we had eaten at on our first date, and then we spent the night in a hotel. My wedding night with Sam was much different than it had been with Frank. Sam was patient and gentle, and until that night, I had no idea that being with a man could be pleasurable and not at all painful. Despite my slight disappointment with the wedding ceremony not being in a church and not getting to wear a white dress, I was happy. I was in love, and life was good. Sam left the next day. I didn't want him to leave on Christmas Day, but he said he had to go. He had to get on the road and get back to work, and because of Aggie's funeral, he was already behind schedule. I hadn't seen him since the day after our wedding, though he often sent me letters. I received at least three each week, sometimes more. I wanted to be able to write him back, but I couldn't as he was traveling and never in the same place for long. I was standing out front talking to my neighbor Karen over the fence on this beautiful morning in late March when a brand-new, bright blue vehicle pulling a brand-new shiny Airstream trailer pulled up in front of the house.

"My goodness, that's fancy," Karen said in her heavy German accent. She had recently moved here with her husband whom she had met while he was serving overseas. She was the same age as I and my only friend, and I, too, was her only friend. The other women in the neighborhood didn't like her because she was from Germany. They all thought her to be a Nazi. I didn't care what others thought—I liked Karen. "Do you know who it is?" she asked.

"No . . ." I started. But then I recognized the man who had stepped out of the vehicle. "Well, actually, yes, it's Sam, my husband."

"So what do you think?" Sam asked as he walked toward me with a huge smile on his face.

"Did you buy this?" I asked, shocked.

"Yes . . . it's ours."

"How, Sam? It must have cost a fortune!"

"Don't worry about the finances," he said, wrapping his arms around me. He kissed me right there in our front yard. And though I was excited to see him, I pulled back, not wanting to kiss out there for all to see. He smiled as he stroked my cheek. "I missed you."

"I missed you too," I replied, smiling.

"Come, you have to see inside," he said as he took my hand and led me over to the camper. He opened the door, and when I stepped inside, I was impressed. It was bigger than I thought it would be. There was a lounge area with a sofa, a small kitchen complete with a stove, oven, and refrigerator. Even a small dining booth. Beyond the kitchen was a tiny bathroom, complete with a shower, sink, and commode. In the very back was a bedroom with a large bed. So large it took up most of the space. I walked back out into the main area looking around again . . . taking in more details this time. The floors were linoleum, and the cabinets were all wood. The countertops were yellow as well as the appliances. The sofa was green as were the curtains. "So what do you think, Anne?" he asked, still smiling.

"I think you're crazy, Sam. It's really nice . . . but . . ."

Stepping forward, he placed his finger over my lips, stopping me from speaking. "I miss you, Anne. I bought this so you can travel with me."

"You want me to go with you?" I asked in a whisper.

He smiled and nodded.

"Hello!" We both turned to see Karen as she popped her head in the door. "May I look?"

"Yes, come on in," Sam said.

"Sam, this is Karen," I said, making introductions. "She's married to Keith. They recently moved in next door."

"It's nice to meet you," Sam said, holding out his hand.

"And you," Karen replied as the two shook. "I was beginning to think that Anne made you up."

"No, I'm real," he replied, smiling.

"Karen, take your time looking," I said, walking over to the door. "I need to speak with Sam privately."

I stepped outside to find several of the other neighbors walking around the vehicle and the trailer, checking it out. I smiled as I walked toward the house. I could hear Sam speaking, telling them they were welcome to look as he followed me inside. "Anne, I didn't do this to upset you," he said once we were both standing inside the house.

"I'm not upset . . . not really."

"But you're not excited," he said, taking my hands in his. "I thought you would be excited about traveling with me."

"Sam, I can't travel with you. I'm pregnant!"

His face went blank, and then a huge smile broke out across his face. "Pregnant?"

"Yes . . . I was sick—or at least I thought I was sick—weeks after you left. So I went to the doctor, and it turns out I'm pregnant. So you see, even if I wanted to travel with you, I can't."

Still smiling, he pulled me close. "What makes you think you can't travel just because you're pregnant? In fact, I'm glad I did this now, knowing you're pregnant. I don't want to miss watching our children grow."

"So are you saying we should raise a family on the road?"

"Yes, for a few years," he replied. "Eventually, when I've made enough money, we can settle down someplace."

"Can we come back and live here?" I asked.

"Here or anywhere you wish," he replied.

***

I closed the cabinet door then stepped back, looking around. It was strange thinking that this trailer was to be to be my home for the next several years. Sam and I had taken what we needed from the house and loaded it into the trailer. The cabinets were now full of cookware and dishes. Decorative pillows and a quilt Aggie had made adorned the sofa. The bathroom had all the essentials. I replaced the bedding that had come with the trailer with yet another quilt that Aggie had made. I even took one of the small braided rugs and placed it on the living room floor. Once the baby came, I knew having a soft floor for him or her to play on would be a good thing. Sam hung a few of my favorite pictures on the wall and brought in a small bookshelf that I filled with as many books as I could possibly fit. With all the things inside, it was no longer spacious, but it was cozy and homey. I smiled. Sam was right . . . I would much rather be living with him in this tight space than having to go months without seeing him.

I picked up my tin box from where I had placed it on the kitchen counter and walked into the bedroom. Sitting on the bed, I opened the lid. I pulled out Mama's ribbon, and I wondered what she would think if she could see me now. Would she be happy for me? That I was married to a good man with a child on the way? I noticed the ribbon was not quite as shiny as it once was, and the edges were beginning to fray. I put it down and picked up the button. Tears instantly formed in my eyes—they always did. No matter the time that passed, my heart still ached for the child I lost. Six . . . my child would be six. It was hard to believe so much time had passed. Next, I picked up the stack of letters with Eric's picture on top. I didn't bother to unbind them but just looked at the picture. I wondered if Eric had lived, would he too have fallen in love by now, been married . . . perhaps even a father himself. He would have been an amazing husband and father to some lucky lady. Setting the letters back inside the tin, I picked up the bus pass that had brought me to Montgomery. I smiled, thinking back on that day and how scared and frightened yet determined I was. Aggie . . . what would I have done had I not met her? I looked at my wedding ring, her ring. I then picked up the hotel key . . . my newest and latest addition to my box. I kept it because that night I gave my body, heart, and soul to Sam. It was a night I always wanted to remember.

"Is that the hotel key I was charged for?"

I looked up, wondering how long Sam had been standing in the doorway watching me. "Yes," I whispered.

As he sat on the bed, he took the key from my hand. I watched silently as he took a moment to look at it. "Why did you keep it?" he asked as he handed it back to me.

"For a memento of that night."

He smiled then looked at my tin. "Are those mementos as well?"

"Yes."

Reaching in, he picked up the stack of letters from Eric. "Your brother?" I nodded. "I can see the resemblance," he said as he put the letters back. He then picked up the bus ticket. He looked at it then set it back down. "What are these memories of?" he asked, pointing to the button and the ribbon.

"I found this button the same day I found out I was pregnant with my first child," I said as tears began to form again. "And the ribbon, it's the only thing I have of my mother's."

"I didn't mean to upset you," he said, reaching out and catching my tears as they fell from my eyes.

"You didn't," I whispered as I set the key back inside the tin and replaced the lid. "No matter how much time passes, my heart still aches for the child I lost."

"I can only imagine. Are you ready?" he asked. "I was going to lock up the house."

"Let me do one last walk-through to make sure we have everything we want," I replied. "Then we can go."

***

September 1946

We had been on the road for six months. I enjoyed traveling and seeing new places and people more than I realized I would. I had no idea the US was as big as it was or how different the terrain varied from one place to another. Even the food and the cultures were different. Most of all, I enjoyed being with Sam. He reminded me of Eric in a lot of ways. He smiled often, and he had one of those personalities that attracted people. Like Eric, Sam was a people person. It was no wonder he was a good salesman. Feeling another pain, this one more intense than the last, I placed my hands on my large belly.

"You alright?" Sam asked, taking his eyes off the road just long enough to glance at me.

"I . . . yes . . . I think perhaps I might be in labor."

He stepped on the brake and slowly stopped the vehicle. "Labor as in the baby is coming?" I nodded. "How long?"

"A few hours . . . I keep having cramps."

"Anne, why didn't you say something when we were in Atlanta?"

"I'm sorry, Sam . . . I wasn't sure . . . I'm still not sure. I haven't done this before!"

He took a deep breath. "Alright . . . stay calm," he said, pulling out a map. "Well," he said a few minutes later, "our best bet will be to head back to Atlanta. I'll find a place to turn around, and we'll go back."

***

Just over an hour later, Sam pulled up to the hospital in Atlanta with our house in tow. It was a good thing, too, for I was definitely in labor. I don't even remember how I got from the vehicle into a room, but somehow, I did. I was immediately hooked up to an IV, and then a nurse came by and shaved me down below—which was an uncomfortable experience, and I had no idea why it was necessary, but even more uncomfortable was the labor pain. It was intense, I had no idea giving birth was so painful. I remember the pain with my first child, but I thought it was painful because something was wrong, I had no idea I would experience so much pain even with a normal, healthy birth. Had I known, I'm not sure I would have been up to the task. After several hours had passed, I finally gave birth to a beautiful baby girl. Agatha Nancy Mathis. She was tiny, skinny, and red with a head full of dark hair just like me. But she was beautiful, perfect, and mine. Once I was decent, Sam was allowed to come into the room to see me. "Did you see her?" I asked as he sat in the chair beside my bed.

"Yes," he said, stroking my hair. "She's beautiful just like her mama," I smiled. "How are you feeling?"

"Tired," I replied.

"Well, I should go and let you rest then."

"No, don't go. I want you to stay here with me for a bit."

***

I opened my eyes when I heard a noise. I must have fallen asleep. I didn't remember doing so, but Sam was gone, the chair beside my bed empty. Looking out the window across the room, it was dark outside. I had been asleep for some time. A woman a few beds down was giving birth. I realized it was her cries that had woken me. The room, which held about twenty beds, was almost full. When the men came home from the war, women everywhere had gotten pregnant. I couldn't see the woman who was giving birth because curtains were pulled around her bed for privacy, but I could hear her. I wondered if I, too, had made that much noise. I could hear a nurse telling her to calm down and be quiet. I felt bad for the woman. Did the nurse not realize how intense the pain of bringing a child into this world was? Maybe she had never experienced it yet herself.

"Anne?" a nurse asked, approaching my bed while pushing a bassinet.

When I looked up, I immediately recognized her. "Marley?" I said, surprised.

She smiled. "Anne?" she said again, and I nodded. "It's so good to see you. "This is you little one?"

"Yes."

"She's precious," Marley said, picking Nancy up then handing her to me.

"I think so," I replied, smiling.

Marley handed me a bottle so I could feed her. "Are you living here in Atlanta now?" she asked.

"No, Sam and I were passing through when I went into labor."

"Sam? He's your husband, I assume?"

"Yes . . . I met him while I was living in Montgomery."

"You still live in Montgomery?" she asked.

"Sort of," I replied. "We have a house there, but Sam is a traveling salesman, and I've been on the road with him."

"Are you going to continue traveling with him now that your baby has arrived?"

"Yes . . . at least that's the plan," I replied.

"It sounds amazing. Have you been many places?"

"All over . . . even as far west as Texas."

"I have always wanted to travel . . . perhaps someday," she said.

"So you're living here in Atlanta now?" I asked.

"Yes, with my sister and her new husband." She paused, reaching out to touch Nancy's little hand. "Six months after I arrived in Atlanta, I received notification that my husband had been killed."

"I am so sorry," I whispered.

Marley smiled as she wiped a tear. "When I received the letter, I decided to stay here with my sister. I got the job here at the hospital, and my sister watches Grace for me while I work."

"How is Grace?" I asked.

"Growing like a weed," she replied, smiling. "She's in second grade this year. Smart like her father too." I smiled and nodded. "Well, I have other patients to check on, but I'll be back in about twenty minutes to take Nancy back to the nursery. It was good seeing you, Anne. And congratulations."

***

July 1947

Nancy was an easy, happy baby, which was good since we lived on the road. It had been ten months since her birth, and we had been traveling all over the east coast, all the way up to Maine. Opening my eyes, I realized we were at a gas station. I didn't see Sam, though I assumed he was inside. I turned, looking into the back seat. Nancy was asleep in her seat with her head lying on her pretend steering wheel. Grabbing her blanket from the seat beside her, I carefully lifted her head, tucking the blanket between her and the steering wheel. She stirred, and I thought I had woken her, but thankfully I hadn't. Turning to face the front once again, I gasped ... I was home ... well, not home anymore, but home as in this was the town I had grown up in. Just then, the car door opened, and Sam got in.

"Hungry?" he said, handing me small brown paper bag. I didn't bother to answer or look inside the bag. I just took it and continued staring out the window. "Babe, what's wrong?" he asked, touching my leg.

"This is home," I whispered.

He looked out the window then back at me. "Like as in the town you were raised in home?" I nodded. "Okay . . . we can go now. I was just stopping for gas, that's all."

"No," I said. "Take me home."

"Are you sure?"

"Yes, I want to see my family."

"Okay, let me drop the trailer off somewhere before we go driving down country lanes. And then we'll get a motel room so we can stay overnight."

***

"There, turn right . . . that's it. That's the house there."

Sam pulled down the long drive, and I stared out the window at the large farmhouse. It was in even worse condition than I had remembered. There were hardly any paint peelings left as the weather had stripped them all away. And the roof was so patched I wondered if it even kept out the rain and snow anymore. Even the barn that Papa had always kept up was looking rough. The fields looked well, but the yard was a mess. Lillian and I had always planted flowers in the spring. Our old flower beds were gone, and grass had grown over them. A barking dog ran up to the car . . . we had never had a dog before. We'd always wanted one, but Mama said no, told us she had enough responsibility with all of us kids. And for some reason, even after she was gone, Papa never got a dog. I wondered if my family was still living here. Surely they had to be. If they had moved, Mary would have told me. We still wrote to each other a couple times a year. Of course, several months had passed since our last exchange of letters.

"You still want to do this?" Sam asked. I looked over at him and nodded. "I'll wait here with Nan . . . unless you want me to come with you."

Nan was Sam's nickname for Nancy. "No, I'll go by myself," I said as I handed Nancy to him. She had woken up from her nap when we had stopped to unload the trailer and get a motel room.

I opened the car door and slowly stepped out. The dog was still barking though he was wagging his tail as he approached. "Hey," I said, kneeling. I held out my hand, and he stopped barking to sniff me. I reached out and pet him. Though I had never had a dog before, our neighbor Karen in Montgomery had three dogs, so I had learned how to interact with them. After petting the dog for a few seconds, I stood. He followed me, still wagging his tail, as I made my way toward the front porch. The front steps were in really rough condition, and I wasn't sure they were even going to hold me. Even the railing on the front porch was loose and missing several pieces. It was sad to see the house in such disrepair. It had never been nice, but it had never been this bad before. I walked up the steps, and thankfully they held. I stood at the door, suddenly very nervous and wondering if I should just turn around and leave. I wanted to see my family, but what would they say about my taking off and leaving without so much as a goodbye? And I felt guilty that I never sent for Lillian. But I was here, and I wasn't sure when or if I would ever be back. So I knocked and waited . . . nothing. I knocked again and almost immediately heard footsteps. The door opened seconds later, and a young lady in a tattered and worn dress with an apron tied around her waist stood before me. She was no more than seventeen. Brown hair, a round face, and blue eyes. It was Helen. "Can I help you?" she said.

"You don't remember me?" I asked. She shook her head. "Helen, it's me, Anne."

"Anne," she whispered. I nodded. She looked at me for a moment longer, and then with tears in her eyes, she threw her arms around me. "Is it really you, Anne?"

"Yes," I whispered. She released me and held me at arm's length, looking me over. I could tell by the look on her face that she noticed my clothes. They were much nicer than hers, and I remembered how I felt once, seeing others dressed so nicely when I was wearing not much more than rags.

"Who is that?" she asked, looking over my shoulder.

I turned around. Sam was standing by the vehicle with Nancy in his arms. "My husband and daughter."

"I heard you were married . . . but I didn't know you had a daughter. Come in, all of you. I want to meet your family."

***

Sam, Nancy, Helen, and I were all sitting around the kitchen table. I kept staring at the light hanging over the table. I knew the house now had electricity running to it as I saw the power lines along the road when we arrived. Still, it was strange. The house was very much the same as I remembered, yet so different. The old wood-burning oven had been replaced by a new electric one. And the icebox, too, was gone, and in its place was a newer refrigerator. There was also a telephone hanging on the wall. I was glad to see the phone. I would now be able to call home from time to time, keep in better contact with Helen and the others. Hearing the back door swing open, I looked that direction just as the twins and Mike entered the kitchen. I knew who they were, but I could tell they didn't recognize me. They were so young when I left home that it didn't surprise me.

"Stay for dinner?" Helen asked after we had all reconnected.

I looked at Sam. "We would love to," he replied.

Sam and the boys then went off into the parlor with Nancy while I helped Helen prepare dinner. "So where is everyone else?" I asked.

"Jeremy is in Pennsylvania. He is at the university."

"University?" I asked, surprised.

Helen smiled and nodded as she continued to shuck the corn. "He's smart, Anne . . . real smart. Studying to be a doctor."

"Lillian?" She didn't answer. "Helen, where is Lillian?"

"She's with Frank," she whispered.

"Frank?" I said, shocked.

She nodded. "Frank was really upset that you left, Anne . . . he told Papa that since you were gone, the debt was no longer paid . . .

Lillian was sent to Frank two weeks after he returned home from the war."

I wiped my tears with the back of my hand. The thought of sweet Lillian living with Frank all these years sickened me. I know he would have touched her, but did he beat her as well, just like he did me? I never thought my leaving would have consequences for Lillian, not like that. "Do you ever see her?" I asked.

"Not often," she replied. "She's busy at her place, and I'm busy here on the farm. It's just me and the boys now."

Where was Papa? I mean, he wasn't here at the moment, but I figured he was in town, or off drinking and gambling. "Where's Papa?" I asked.

"Papa's dead, Anne. He died several years ago."

"Dead?" I said, setting down the potato peeler I held in my hands. Helen nodded. No wonder the house was in such a state. Three teen boys were running the farm on their own. "How . . . how did Papa die?"

"The doctor said it was most likely cancer. He got sick so suddenly and died within just a few weeks."

"Mary never told me," I said, mostly to myself.

"Jeremy told her not to," Helen replied. "Papa died just months after you left. Jeremy didn't want you to come home . . . you had gotten away, Anne. You have a good life, and you're happy . . ."

I wrapped my arms around Helen, who was now crying. "I'm sorry, I'm so sorry I left you all."

"No, Anne," she said, pushing me away. "Don't be sorry. I know why you left, and I would have, too, if I had been in your situation."

She went back to shucking corn, and I picked up the potato peeler and began peeling potatoes once again. "Why are you still here, Helen?" I asked.

"Someone needed to stay with the boys. Besides, I'm happy, Anne. I don't mind this life. I'm engaged," she said, holding out her hand and smiling.

It was the first time I noticed the ring on her finger. It was plain, simple but pretty. "Is he nice?"

Helen blushed. "Yes," she whispered.

"Is he from around here?"

She nodded. "He's a teacher at the local high school. We met at a church function."

"You go to church now?" I asked, surprised.

"After Papa died, I started going. The boys go too. Walter . . . that's my fiancé's name, he's going to move in here after we're married. He's going to fix the house up. He's the one who purchased all the new appliances for me. I even have an electric washing machine—I'll show it to you after dinner. It's amazing. And Walter said that once he has saved up enough money, he's going to have a washroom put in the house! Can you imagine, Anne, a washroom . . . right here in the house? Why, I guess you can. With all the traveling you've done, all the hotels you've stayed at, I'm sure you've seen many washrooms. Still, the idea of not having to boil water for a bath . . ."

I smiled as Helen went on and on. I was glad to hear she was happy, that she had found someone to love, someone who loved her. And I was glad to hear that the house was going to receive care too.

"You'll be able to meet Walter. He'll be here tonight. He eats dinner with us most every night. You know, Papa is buried in the cemetery next to Mama. You should go see them—Eric, too—after dinner . . . I would be glad to watch Nancy for you."

***

I knelt before my parents' graves. I had no tears. I hadn't cried over Mama for several years now. My heart still ached for her, but it was so long ago when she died, and I was so young that it was a distant memory. And Papa . . . well, we were never very close. He was my papa, and for that I loved him. Still, I was angry, not only because he sent me away, but also for Lillian. How could he? Hearing footsteps, I turned to see Sam approaching. "Take your time," he said as I stood to my feet.

"I'm done," I whispered.

I stepped over and looked at Eric's grave one last time, for I had visited with him first. Oh, how I missed him.

"I wish you could have met him, Sam. He would have liked you. And I know the two of you would have gotten along well."

"I'm sorry I never had the chance to meet him," he said as he placed his arm around me.

"Helen told me that my papa sent my sister Lillian to Frank," I said as we began to walk through the cemetery toward the car. "How could he, Sam?"

"I don't know, Anne," he replied. "I don't know how a father could do such a horrible thing to his own children."

"I want to see Lillian, but I'm afraid to face him."

"Then I'll go with you. Tomorrow," he said. "We can leave Nancy with Helen again. I'm sure she won't mind . . . I'll take you."

I smiled and nodded, looking up at Sam. Helen was watching Nancy for us right now—she had insisted. And I knew she would gladly watch her for us tomorrow so I could go visit Lillian.

***

Tomorrow could not come soon enough, and yet it came too soon. I hadn't slept well all night as I was excited to see Lillian, but as much as I was excited, I was frightened as well. What would I find? And how would I feel about seeing Frank? Perhaps I wouldn't see him at all. Maybe he would be out in the field or in town. The closer we got to his farm, the more nervous I became.

"I can turn around," Sam said.

I looked at him. He had obviously detected my nervousness. "No, I need to see her. Turn right here," I said, pointing. Sam turned, and we started down the lane, passing Mary's house first. As we passed the second house, I saw five children playing in the front yard and a middle-aged woman sitting on a porch swing watching them. A new family must have moved in. When I had lived here, a widower lived in the house. He was very reclusive. Then I remembered Mary writing in one of her letters to me that he had passed. "This is the house," I said in a whisper.

Sam pulled into the drive, and as we neared the house, I saw a small boy sitting on the front porch playing with a toy. The house looked the same as I remembered. It was tidy, clean, and in great condition, a stark contrast to my childhood home. A young woman came out the front door with an infant in her arms followed by a little girl. It was Lillian. I opened the car door and had only taken a few steps when she recognized me. "Anne," she called out as she quickly made her way toward me.

We embraced, and we cried. "Mama, you okay?" the little girl asked, now tugging on Lillian's skirts.

"I'm fine, baby," she replied. "Here, take your sister inside. I'll be in shortly." Lillian then turned. "Eric, you go inside as well," she called out. I smiled, watching as the young boy stood and followed his sister into the house.

"You named him after Eric," I said. She nodded. "They're beautiful, Lillian."

"I have two more boys. They're with their father right now."

"Five ... you have five children?" She nodded, and I was shocked. Lillian was nineteen and already had five children.

"I think Frank keeps me pregnant so I won't leave."

"I'm sorry, Lillian," I whispered.

"Don't be. It's not your fault. Truth is, if I didn't have so many children, I would leave. I would have left years ago, just like you did. Is that your husband?" she asked, looking over my shoulder.

Looking behind, I saw Sam standing by the car just watching us. "Yes," I replied, turning back around to face Lillian.

Lillian smiled. "Mary told me you had married. And you have a daughter?"

"Yes, Nancy ... she's with Helen right now. I didn't bring her ... I was afraid to bring her ... not sure what I would find."

"I would have loved to have met her, but I understand," she said.

"I would like to visit my baby's grave . . . is he here?"

"No, Frank is in town," she replied.

"Walk to the grave with me then?" She nodded and linked her arm in mine. "We'll be right back," I shouted to Sam.

He nodded, and the two of us walked silently around the house over to the tree where the grave was. I smiled as we neared. The weeds had been pulled, and there were flowers. They were wilted, and I could tell they had been here for several days. Still, my baby had not been forgotten. I looked at Lillian.

"I come out here from time to time," she said. "I feel close to you when I'm here. Besides, if this was my child, I would want to know someone cared."

"Thank you," I said with tears falling down my face.

She nodded, and I dropped to my knees, running my hand over the grass as if to touch my child. I don't know if having Nancy helped to dull the pain or intensify it. Before I had Nancy, I really had no idea what it was like to be a mother, to actually hold my child in my arms and watch her grow. How much I had missed. All the milestones I would never see, the birthdays that never happened.

"Lillian, come with us," I said, looking up at her. "Your children too."

"Anne, I can't."

"Does he hurt you?"

"He used to," she said, dropping to her knees beside me. "Shortly after Jeremy got home, he saw some bruises I had. I tried to lie, to hide it, but he didn't believe me. Jeremy beat the crap out of Frank, and I honestly thought he was going to kill him. Frank was bedridden for several days after. Jeremy told Frank that if he ever touched me again, he would kill him. Frank must have believed him because he hasn't hit me since. I can't go ,Anne. This is my life . . . my cross to bear. It's not all bad. I have my children, and I have the Lord."

"You too," I whispered.

"Oh, Anne, don't push God away. He loves you so very much."
She reached out and touched the simple headstone. "I have often
thought that if this child had lived, you would still be here. Married
to Frank." I nodded. I, too, knew that to be true. I wouldn't have left
Frank if our baby had lived. Lillian smiled at me. "Your baby is with
God, and someday you will be reunited." Tears came pouring down
her face as they did mine. "God allowed this child to be taken from
you because he had other plans for you, Anne. Don't you ever regret
leaving, don't you feel sorry for me, and don't you ever come back
here again. You leave this small town . . . there is nothing here for
you. Jeremy knows that . . . he left, and I doubt he will ever return.
You go, Anne, and you live your life to the fullest."

***

Just as Lillian and I arrived back at the car, a truck pulled into the
drive. Frank's truck. "You go now," Lillian said, hugging me. "You
go and remember what I said."

"I'll write," I said.

"Yes, please do. And when you're settled somewhere, I'll write
you."

She released me just as Frank stepped out of his truck. Two
young boys jumped out of the bed of the truck. They looked just like
Frank, but I could tell they had Lillian's spirit. Frank walked around
the front of his truck and stopped when he saw me. He stood staring
at me with his one good eye . . . looking at me as if he had seen a
ghost. The boys stood at his side, staring as well, thought I could tell
they were just curious as to who Sam and I were. I had often
wondered how bad Frank's wound was—not that I cared, but I
wondered out of curiosity. He had a patch over his right eye, making
him look sort of like a pirate. And the right side of his face was
scarred from where the fire had burned him. I noticed his neck had
burn marks as well. He didn't scare me like I thought he would.
Perhaps it was because Sam was here, because I knew Sam would
never let Frank hurt me.

"Let's go, Anne," Sam said, taking my arm and then helping me into the vehicle.

I sat, and Sam closed the door. Frank's gaze was on me the entire time Sam walked around our vehicle. As we pulled away, I waved to Lillian. I hated leaving her here, but at least Frank wasn't hurting her anymore. Sam was quiet the entire ride back into town. I wondered what he was thinking, or perhaps he was just letting me think.

***

We stayed in town two more days so I could see Mary and spend more time with my siblings. I didn't see Lillian again while we were in town, though we wrote letters to each other, just like we promised. And like my childhood home, she and Frank now had electricity running to their house as well as a telephone, so Lillian and I called each other every year on our birthdays. It was twelve years later that I went home again. Unfortunately, it was not a happy reunion. My reason for returning home was Lillian. Frank had lost his temper, and in a drunken rage, he had pushed her down the stairs. She was pregnant at the time, and both Lillian and her baby died. She didn't die immediately—it took several days—and I was there at her bedside when she passed. Lillian and her baby were buried together in the cemetery next to Eric. Frank was arrested and ended up being sentenced, sent to prison for fourteen years though I heard he only served five of them before he was released. I never saw Frank again. Helen and her husband Walter took in Lillian's youngest children, the ones who still lived at home at the time of her death, and they raised them along with their own four children. As life happened, Frank was not the only man I knew who served time.

SEVEN

September 1949

"Look, Mama!"

"Wow, look at that tower," I said, looking up from the book I was reading.

"I did it," Nancy said, smiling, proud of the block tower she had made. I smiled with her . . . she had just turned three. I don't know where the years had gone, where my baby had gone. It seemed as if I had awakened one morning, and my baby was becoming a little girl. Seconds later, she knocked her tower down. We were still living in the trailer, traveling, but at the moment, we were in Birmingham, Alabama. We came to Birmingham about every three months. Whenever we were here, Sam would stay at a hotel in town while I stayed with Helen at a nearby campground. He would pop in from time to time, but whenever we were in Birmingham, work kept him so busy we didn't see much of him. The timer rang, and I set my book down on the sofa.

"Eat, Mama?" Nancy asked as I stood and walked into the kitchen.

"Yes, baby, we're going to eat dinner soon," I replied as I opened the oven door.

I peeked in at the casserole. It was definitely done, so I grabbed a couple of hot pads and removed it. Just as I set the casserole on the stove, there was a knock on the door. I closed the oven door and turned it off, tossing the hot pads onto the counter before walking the short distance from the kitchen to the door, wondering who it could be. I knew it wasn't Sam—he would have just walked right in. Two men in suits stood outside, and another man stood by a black car parked at the end of our camping spot. I looked down as Nancy wrapped her little arms around my legs. "Are you Anne Smith?"

"Anne Mathis," I replied, looking back up. "My maiden name was Smith."

The two men looked at each other. "We need you to come with us," one of them said.

"What do you mean?" I asked.

"We have to ask you a few questions," the other man said as he held up a badge.

They were some kind of law enforcement officers. "Am I in trouble?"

"Ma'am, we can't talk here."

"Mama," Nancy said.

I could tell she was frightened, and I bent over and picked her up. "May we talk here . . . my daughter?"

"She can come too."

"Alright, let me grab my purse."

"No," the man said, taking hold of my arm. "You just need to come with us."

Now I was frightened. But I silently did as asked, trying to stay calm for Nanny's sake as I exited the camper and followed the men to the car. I noticed another car sitting not too far away. As I got into the car, four men stepped out of the second vehicle and began walking toward my trailer. I sat nervously watching as I held Nancy on my lap.

"Dolly, Mama," she cried out. Nancy never went anywhere without her baby doll that she had so aptly named Dolly. The car pulled off just as the men entered the trailer. What were they doing in my trailer? "Dolly, I want Dolly!"

"Baby, I'm sorry," I said, kissing the top of her head. "We left Dolly at home. You can get her later." Nancy cried and cried. She cried all the way to the local police station. I wanted to cry too because I had no idea what was going on or why those men had entered our home. But I didn't cry. I had to be strong for Nancy.

"Am I under arrest?" I asked as I was led into the building.

"At this point, no, but we shall see," a man replied.

My heart began to beat fast. What was happening? Why was I even here? I had never broken the law, not that I knew of. And where was Sam? Surely they would have contacted Sam. As soon as I stepped into the lobby, a woman who was sitting in a row of chairs on the far wall stood and approached. "I'll take the child," she said, reaching out.

Holding tightly to Nancy, I stepped back.

"Give her the child, ma'am," one of the men said before I'd even had a chance to speak. "When we're done questioning you, she'll be returned."

I didn't want to give Nancy up, but I knew I had no choice. I forced a smile and looked at Nancy. "You go with this nice lady, and Mama will see you soon."

"No, Mama," she said, wrapping her little arms tightly around my neck.

The woman reached over, snatching her from my arms. Nancy screamed and reached out for me. "Her name is Nancy," I called after the woman as she was leaving with Nancy. "And she's probably hungry—it's past her dinnertime."

"Hey," the man said, grabbing my arm. "Don't worry about your daughter. Come this way." Still holding my arm, he led me down the hall into a small room. There was nothing but a table, two chairs, and a light hanging from the ceiling above that flickered every so often. "Sit," he demanded, releasing my arm. I got the feeling that he did not like me very much, but I had no idea why. I walked over to one of the chairs and sat. He took a seat in the chair across from mine. The other man was in the room as well, though he was standing by the door. I sat quietly while the man lit a cigarette. "When did you first meet Samuel Mathis?" he asked as he set several files onto the table.

"About six years ago . . . he had just returned from the war. He was released early due to an injury he sustained while overseas."

"What do you know if his illegal activities?"

"Illegal activities? I don't—"

"Do you want to see your daughter again?" he yelled as he released a breath of smoke right into my face.

"Of course I do," I said.

"Then you better talk. We know you're involved." Hearing the door open behind me, I turned around to look, hoping it was Sam. It wasn't. Another strange man entered the room. He was dressed differently than the other two, though, and I realized he was one of the local authorities. "Now, Ms. Smith, let's try this again," the man said, bringing my attention back to him.

"Mathis," I said. He shot me a nasty look as he took another puff of his cigarette. "Smith is my maiden name. Sam and I were married almost four years ago."

"Married?"

"Yes, that's what I said."

"Well, how is that possible, Ms. Smith? Samuel Mathis is already married. He was married back in 1936 to a Sarah Gardner."

"No, you must have the wrong man then," I said. "My Sam has never been married before."

He pulled a document from the folder and slid it across the table. Reaching out, I took it and spun it around. Clipped to the front was a picture of a young man and even younger woman standing in front of a church. It was Sam . . . my Sam. Younger, but no doubt him. Flipping the picture, I was now looking at a marriage certificate, and Sam's signature was at the bottom. I looked up as tears formed in my eyes.

"You ready to talk yet?" the man asked.

"I never said I wouldn't talk," I replied.

***

I was questioned for several hours, left alone for a couple hours, then questioned again. And I was asked the same questions over and over. And each time, I gave the same answers . . . I knew nothing. I was tired, hungry, and thirsty. My head was spinning, and I had to use the restroom as well. They had only let me go one other time, and that was hours ago now. Most of all, I was worried about Nancy. Where was she, and was she okay? On top of everything else, I was hurt. Everything I knew about Sam was a lie. Not only was he married to another woman, but he had also been stealing money. He was not a salesman—he was a thief. The door opened, and I lifted my head off the table. It was an officer, the one who had been silently watching as the men in suits questioned me. "Come on," he said. "You are free to go."

"My daughter?" I asked as I stood.

"She's waiting for you in the lobby."

I nodded as I quickly made my way over to the door. I was glad to leave this room, and I prayed I never had to see it again. "I need to . . ." I said, stopping in front of the restroom.

"I understand," he said.

When I came out of the restroom, the man was still waiting for me. "I assume you believed me. That's why you're letting me go?" He nodded. "And Sam?"

"He's going to be prosecuted, and most likely he'll be locked up for a very long time."

"Is he here?" I asked. He nodded. "May I see him?" The man began to shake his head. "Please . . . let me talk to him."

"Alright, but I will be in the room with you the entire time."

"I understand," I said.

"This way."

I followed the officer just a short distance down the hall. He opened the door, and I entered a room that looked very similar to the one I had been held in. "Anne!" Sam said, standing while quickly putting out his cigarette.

"Stay sitting," the man said, voice slightly raised.

Sam sat back down, and I walked over to the table, taking the seat across from him. It was strange being in this chair, on this side . . . the one asking the questions now. He opened his mouth to speak, and I cut him off.

"How could you, Sam? How could you? Married? You were married? Do you have any idea what I've been through these last several hours? Nancy was taken from me, and I've been questioned over and over. These men look at me like trash . . . they treat me like a woman with no morals. All this time I thought we were married . . . but we aren't, are we?"

"No."

I closed my eyes. Two men . . . I had been with two men in my life, both of whom I thought I was married to, only to find out I was never married to either one of them. Sam, though, he had me sign something. I should have read it, but I didn't, for I trusted him. "What did I sign, Sam. It wasn't a marriage license, was it?"

"No, it was Aggie's estate."

My heart sank. I had planned on taking Nancy and going back to Montgomery. Now I had nowhere to go. "You took the house from me?"

He nodded. "How do you think I paid for the vehicle and the trailer? I sold the house."

"And the money?" I asked.

"The money is still there, but the FBI seized it. You won't have access to it. And even if I did still own the house, that would have been taken too, seeing as you signed everything over into my name."

I sat silently, just staring at him for several seconds. "Why?"

"Sarah and I . . . I had known her since we were kids," he said. "We were both young and stupid. I knocked her up then married her because it was the right thing to do."

"And Aggie didn't know?"

"No, I never told her," he explained. "She had no idea I was married or that I had any children."

"You have other children?" I asked, shocked. He nodded. "How many?"

"Four, three with Sarah and Nancy."

More tears fell from my eyes. "Then why did you marry me, Sam, or pretend to anyway? Why did you even ask me out knowing you were married?"

"Because I never loved Sarah . . . I tried, but I didn't. You were pretty, sweet . . . and the truth is, I never planned on falling in love with you either. I thought perhaps we would go on a few dates, and that would be the end of it, but it wasn't. I fell in love with you, Anne. Then Aggie died, and I didn't want to lose you. I couldn't marry you, not legally, so I lied."

"That's why you didn't want a church wedding," I whispered. He nodded. "Were you ever going to tell me?"

"No. In fact, after I had enough money, I was planning on moving us to California, starting new . . . never having to see Sarah again."

It was then I realized that Sam was not working every time we were in Birmingham . . . he was with his other family. Who was this man who lied to not only me but to this other woman? Who would leave his children, his own flesh and blood? Who would steal money from people? He reached out for my hand.

"Don't touch me," I said, quickly pulling away.

"Anne, please," he said. "Please, Anne, hear me out!"

"No, you hear me out, Sam! You're a liar and a thief. You took everything from me . . . my livelihood and my good name. The only good thing that came out of this mess is our daughter." I stood from the chair. "You once told me that you would never hurt me . . . well, you did, Sam, because this hurts. I gave you my heart, and you threw it away." I then turned and walked away.

"Anne, please at least tell me where you're going," he called out. "Anne! Anne! I need to know where you're taking Nancy! Anne, I'm sorry. I love you, Anne . . . Anne!"

I left the room, and even with the door shut, I could hear Sam calling for me. I stood in the hall and took a moment to compose myself as I wiped my tears away. "Thank you," I said to the officer.

"No problem," he replied sympathetically. "Come on, your daughter is waiting for you."

I entered the lobby and immediately saw Nancy sitting in a chair beside the woman. "Mama!" she squealed as she scooted off the chair.

She ran to me, and I picked her up and squeezed her tightly, taking in a deep breath of her scent as I did. I had never been separated from her before, and I prayed that never again would we be apart. "Come, I'll give you a ride," the officer said a minute later.

We had not taken but a few steps when a woman entered the lobby from the opposite hall. Her face was red and puffy, and I could tell she, too, had been crying. "Is that her?" she said to the man in the suit that was standing beside her, her voice echoing in the large lobby. "It this the slut who ruined my marriage?" The man nodded, and before I realized what was happening, the woman walked over and slapped me across the face. "You fornicating whore!"

Nancy began to cry, and the officer beside me reached out, putting himself between the other woman and myself. I tried to calm Nancy down as the woman continued yelling obscenities at me. Finally, the men in suits hauled her away, and I heard them comforting her with their words. The officer grabbed my arm and quickly led me outside. I could tell from the sun that it was late afternoon. I had been at the station for almost twenty-four hours.

"I apologize," he said, handing me his handkerchief. I looked at him. "Your lip, it's bleeding."

"Oh," I said, taking the handkerchief and blotting my lip. Sure enough, I was bleeding. "Thank you," I said when I was done, holding out his handkerchief to him.

"Keep it." I nodded. "My car is over here," he said.

"I can't blame her," I said once we were sitting in the car. "I can understand why she's so upset . . . why she would take her anger out on me. She's hurt."

"So are you," the officer replied. "And yet you didn't lose your cool."

***

We drove silently the rest of the way to the trailer. Once inside, I was shocked. It was a mess. It looked as if a storm had passed through. The cushions and pillows had been thrown off the sofa. All the books from my bookshelf were scattered on the floor. The kitchen cabinets were all opened, and every shelf was disturbed. The oven door was open, and even the racks had been removed and thrown carelessly onto the floor. The uneaten casserole still sat undisturbed on the stovetop, the only thing I could see that was untouched. "Thank you for the ride," I said, turning to look at the officer.

"You need to pack a bag, take only the essentials," he said.

"I don't understand," I replied, confused.

"Everything Sam owned was seized. You can't stay here. I'm not even supposed to let you remove anything, but I just don't have the heart to send you and your daughter off without at least the basics." I nodded. "Here," he said reaching out. "Let me hold her while you pack."

I handed Nancy to the officer, expecting her to cry once again, but she didn't. I then walked into the bedroom. I could hear him talking to her, and I wondered if he had any children of his own. The bedroom, too, was a mess. The mattress had been flipped off the bed, and our clothing was everywhere. I saw my tin on the floor in the corner. Its contents had been dumped onto the floor, and the letters from Eric and the postcards were scattered all about the room. With tears falling, I dropped to my knees and began gathering up the letters. Once I had picked them all up, including the picture of Eric, I set them in the tin. I could not find the rubber band—I would find another one later. I picked up all my postcards, then the ribbon, the ticket, and the key, and I put them all back into my tin. The button, where was my button? I frantically looked all over the floor. Lifting one of Sam's shirts, I breathed out a sigh of relief. There was my button. Picking it up, I held it close for just a moment before I placed it in the tin. Once the lid was secured, I set the tin on the bed. I found a bag and began to collect the clothing we would need. I found three dresses of mine along with a cardigan. I gathered up some undergarments, and a sudden feeling of shame and embarrassment came over me as I did. I realized that men had seen them, that they had gone through my personal things. I found five outfits for Nancy, then I quickly folded everything, placing all the items into the bag. I went into the bathroom and picked up our toothbrushes. I stood looking at Sam's toothbrush, now sitting alone in the holder. It was over, my life . . . the life I knew. It had all been a lie, and it was over. Holding back tears, I took a deep breath. Gathering a few more items I would need, I brought everything back into the room and placed them into the bag. Then, picking up the bag, I walked back out into the main area. The officer had placed the cushion back on the couch and was sitting with Nancy on his lap, looking at a picture book with her. Setting the bag on the kitchen counter, I looked for the can that Sam and I kept cash in. Surprisingly it was still in the cabinet. Grabbing it down, I pulled off the lid. Disappointment . . . it was empty.

"Looking for something?" the officer asked.

"Money," I said, setting the can onto the counter. "It's gone."

"I'm sure the men took it. I'm sorry," he whispered. "You ready then?"

I nodded, picked up the bag, and walked over to the door. The officer followed me outside, still holding Nancy. "Wait," I said, turning around.

I quickly ran back inside and looked all around the living area. Then, seeing Dolly's feet peeking out from under some books on the floor, I snatched her up. When I stepped back outside, Nancy, seeing Dolly in my hands, smiled. "Dolly," she squealed.

I smiled as I handed Dolly to her. She held Dolly close and squeezed her tight. "You ready then?" the officer asked, smiling as well.

"Yes," I replied. "Where are we going?" I asked as I followed him to the car.

"To the bus station. I'm going to purchase you tickets home."

"Home?"

"Virginia. You have family there if I recall," he said.

I nodded. He opened the car door for me, and once I was sitting, he handed Nancy to me. She was the only one who talked during the ride back into town. She was happy this time around as she had Dolly. Once at the bus station, the officer purchased two tickets to my hometown in Virginia, and I wondered just how much information he knew about me. What exactly did they know?

"Come with me," he said, turning from the ticket booth with tickets in hand.

I followed him back outside where we crossed the street. "Where are we going now?" I asked curiously.

"To a motel. Your bus doesn't leave until the morning," he replied. I nodded then continued following him.

I wasn't sure how far we were going to walk. I was exhausted, and Nancy was getting heavy in my arms. Thankfully, the officer was carrying my bag for me. Two blocks later, we entered a five-story building that had seen better days.

"Wait here," he said to me once we were in the lobby. I stood holding Nancy and looking around while the officer talked to the man at the front desk. The furniture was old and faded, the fabric completely worn through on several of the sofas. Though it was day and there were lights, it was fairly dark inside. Of course, the dark maroon and green colors did not help. A few older men were sitting around, smoking cigars, each reading a newspaper. "Follow me," the officer said, getting my attention. I followed him silently up a set of stairs to the third floor, then down a long narrow hall where he stopped at the last door on the right. He unlocked the door and held it open for me, and I stepped inside. The room was small and had a musty smell, but I wasn't going to complain. I was exhausted and just wanted to get some rest. As I put Nancy down, he set my bag on the bed. "Here you go," he said, handing me the tickets and the room key.

"Thank you," I replied as I took them.

He then removed his wallet and took out some cash. "The room is already paid for," he said, offering me the money. "This is for food."

"Thank you," I said once again as I took the money.

I looked down. He had given me two dollars. "Your bus leaves at 10:30 tomorrow." I nodded, looking back up at him. "And I'm sorry . . . about how things turned out. I know the others didn't treat you very kindly, but you were a victim just as much as any of the others Sam hurt. You take care of yourself." I nodded, and he turned to leave.

"Wait!" I called out. Stopping at the door, he turned around. "I never got your name."

"Mark."

"Thank you, Mark. Thank you for everything."

"No problem . . . I didn't think to stop and get you anything to eat. I'm sure you and your daughter are hungry."

"You gave me some money," I said, holding it up.

"Well, that's for your travels. There's a diner just across the street. I'll run over, grab something for you, and bring it back."

"Thank you," I said as he left.

***

With how exhausted I was and a full stomach, I slept hard that night and woke the next morning feeling much better—well, as good as I could under the circumstances. I was still numb, still in shock, and still wondering how this had happened. One day life was going so well, and the next day it came crashing down all around me. After taking a bath and bathing Nancy, I checked out of the hotel. I then took Nancy across the street to the diner for breakfast. Not only had Mark brought dinner for us last night, but he also brought a coloring book and crayons for Nancy. So she was coloring while we ate, and I sat thinking. I couldn't go home, not with Frank there. The town was too small, and I was bound to run into him. And though I wanted to see Lillian, Helen, Mary, and the others, I just couldn't do it. And it wasn't just because Frank was there . . . if I was being completely honest with myself, it was because I was ashamed. They all thought I was doing well, and I thought I was too until just a couple days ago. And besides that, Helen and Walter had recently gotten married. They didn't need Nancy and me to come in and interrupt their lives. No, I couldn't go home. I didn't want my family to know I had failed. It was 9:30 when we finished eating, and though we had a bit of time before our bus left, I decided to head over to the bus depot. Once inside, I walked over to a wall that had a map of the US with all the bus routes. Where would I go? Perhaps I should go to Pennsylvania. Last I heard, Jeremy was there, still in medical school. But then I remember in the last letter I had received from Helen, that Jeremy, too, was recently married. No, not only did he have his own family to worry about now, if I showed up at his door, he would know I had failed. So I stood looking at the map for a good ten minutes, holding Nancy close, wondering what to do. I had two tickets and less than two dollars to my name and a three-year-old child to care for. Sam had taken us to the beach once in the Carolinas, and I remembered it was beautiful. I needed something beautiful in my life right now, so I turned around and made my way over to the ticket booth.

"May I help you?" the man behind the window asked.

"Yes, I want to exchange these tickets," I said as I pushed them through the slot in the window toward him.

He picked them up and looked at them. "So where do you want to go?"

"Charleston. Charleston, South Carolina."

EIGHT

I stepped off the bus and took a deep breath. We had arrived in Charleston, and there was no turning back for I did not have enough money to go anywhere else. It was early morning, and it was a beautiful fall day, I was glad it wasn't too cold as I took Nancy's hand and began to walk down the street. I had no idea where I was going or what I was going to do, but I knew I had to find a job and a place to stay. I soon found myself walking down a tree-lined street with huge mansions. I couldn't even imagine living in such majesty, and I thought perhaps this was what heaven looked like. The lawns were pristine, and the cars in the driveways were fancy. As we walked past the homes, I caught a glance of the people. They, too, were dressed all fancy. I looked at my dress and then at Nancy's. We had nice clothing—Sam had always given me money to buy store-bought dresses for Nancy and myself—but compared to the ladies who lived in these houses, we were plain. I remembered Helen looking at my dress when I had last seen her. She too must have felt so plain. I should have given her a couple of my dresses while I was there Lillian too. I don't know why I didn't think to do so at the time. Nancy and I turned down yet another tree-lined street of big fancy homes, and I saw an older woman pruning a rose bush by the white picket fence that surrounded her yard. Her house, too, was large, but there was something about her that attracted me, that made her seem approachable when the others weren't.

"Good morning," I said as I approached.

"Good morning," she replied, looking up and smiling.

"I was wondering if you knew of anyone who might be looking for help."

"What are you looking to do?"

"I can clean, cook, watch children, sew just about anything . . ."

"Your flowers are pretty," Nancy said, interrupting me.

The woman looked down at Nancy and smiled. She cut a rose off the bush, cut off the thorns, and handed the rose over the fence to Nancy. "For you, young lady."

"Thank you," Nancy replied shyly in a voice barely above a whisper.

The woman, still smiling, then looked back at me. "She's a beautiful little girl." I nodded, smiling. "You might want to try Miss Janice," she then said. "She lives on the next block over. Hers is the peach-colored house with black shutters. You can't miss it. I heard just last week that she was looking for some help around the house."

"Thank you," I said, smiling as Nancy took off skipping and dancing down the sidewalk with her prized flower.

"Good luck," the old woman called after me as I took off after Nancy.

***

It was four thirty, and I had been out looking for a job all day. I couldn't find one. I had gone first to Miss Janice's house. She had no work for me but gave me the name of another person, who in turn gave me yet another name. Many put on fake smiles and sent me off with a name, though others came right out and told me why exactly they would not hire me. No one wanted to hire a single woman, especially one with a child.

"Mama, I'm hungry."

I looked down at Nancy. She was hungry, but I could tell she was tired too. She hadn't gotten a nap today, and aside from the few crackers I had given her hours earlier, we had not eaten all day. "Alright baby," I said, picking her up. "Let's get some dinner."

A few blocks later, I turned the corner and began walking down a sidewalk that had several businesses to my left and the beach across the street to my right. I set Nancy down—I could no longer carry her and our bag. I stood listening to the sound of the ocean. It was soothing.

"What's that, Mama?" Nancy asked, pointing to the beach.

She was so young the last time we were here that she didn't remember. "It's the ocean. baby. I'll take you to see it soon." She nodded and smiled, holding tight to Dolly. "Come along," I said as we began to walk once again. I was beginning to get scared. I didn't realize it would be this hard to find employment. And where were we going to sleep tonight? We came to a diner, and right away I noticed a help wanted sign in the window. I didn't expect to get the job, but we did have to eat, so I opened the door.

"Sit anywhere," a voice yelled upon hearing the bell on the door as Nancy and I entered.

Aside from one other customer who was sitting at the bar, the diner was empty. I took a quick look around and chose a booth in the far corner by the window so Nancy could look outside at the ocean. Grabbing a menu that was tucked behind the napkin dispenser, I looked it over. A few minutes later, a woman approached. "Are you ready to order?" she asked, pulling a notepad and pencil from her apron.

"Yes, please. We will have the American cheese sandwich with fries."

"To drink?"

"Water for me, please, and milk for her."

"It will be out shortly," she said as she walked off.

Ten minutes later, our food arrived. As we ate, more and more people came in, and the once empty diner was now bustling. I also noticed that the woman who had served us was the only waitress, and she was struggling to keep up with all the tables. "Would you like any dessert," she asked as she came by to collect our empty plate.

"Yes," Nancy answered.

The woman smiled at Nancy then looked at me. "What do you recommend?" I asked.

"The peach cobbler," she replied.

"We will try that then."

"I'll have it right out," she said as she rushed off.

Nancy smiled, and I smiled back. "You were such a good girl today I figured you deserved a treat."

"Yes, I was, Mama. I'm always good."

I gave her a quick squeeze, smiling once again just as the woman set the cobbler in front of us. About twenty minutes later, she brought the check by.

"Is the owner here?" I asked.

"Yes, he is in the back. Why?"

"Well, I saw the help wanted sign, and I'm looking for a job." The woman looked at Nancy. "I know . . . she won't be a problem, I promise. I need the work. I'm desperate."

She stood looking at me for a few seconds, though it seemed so much longer. "Alright, follow me," she said.

"Nancy, you stay here with our bag. You sit and play with Dolly like a big girl," I said as I took her coloring book and crayons out and set them on the table. "You may color too."

"Okay, Mama," she replied as I scooted out of the bench and quickly followed the woman behind the bar.

"Put this on," the woman said, handing me an apron.

"You mean, I'm hired? I'm to start now?"

"I can't hire you. That's Adam's decision. But you prove yourself tonight, and my guess is the job will be yours." I smiled as I tied the apron around my waist. "Here," she said, handing me a pad and pencil. "You take all those tables along that wall."

***

Although the diner served all sorts of clientele, most were men, and I quickly learned that with a smile and little flirting, I could make good tips. The place was busy from five all the way until closing at nine. Not once did I have time for a break. Thankfully Nancy sat quietly until she fell asleep at about seven thirty. I was cleaning off my last table when a man approached. He looked to be in his fifties. His dark hair was mixed with gray in places. His shirt was covered in grease stains. He was the cook, but it was then that I realized he was also the owner. "Your name is Anne?"

"Yes," I replied.

"That's your daughter?" he asked, looking over at the booth in the back where Nancy was still sound asleep.

"Yes."

"Where's your husband?" he asked, looking down at my hand.

I bit my lip, not knowing what to say. I really needed this job. "He is no longer around."

"Well, you did really well tonight. So if you can find a place for your daughter to stay while you work, the job is yours."

I smiled excitedly. Then my smiled faded as I realized I had no place to live, let alone did I know anyone who could watch my daughter. "I just moved here, sir," I said. "I don't know anyone. May I please have a few days to find someone to watch her? She won't be any trouble. I swear."

He stood looking at me for a few seconds, and I prayed the entire time he would give me a chance. "I'll give you a few days."

"Thank you," I replied, smiling once again.

"See you tomorrow, Anne . . . 5:30 in the morning," he said as he left.

I finished cleaning my table, removed my apron, then looked at the money I had made. Still not enough for a hotel, so I had no idea where I was going to go. "Here," Pam, the other waitress said, getting my attention.

"What's this?" I asked as she handed me some more money.

"Your wages," she replied. "We get paid every night." I couldn't believe it—I now had enough money to get a room for the night. Relieved, I walked over to the booth where Nancy was sleeping and put the money in my bag. I picked up her coloring book and crayons and placed them into the bag as well. As I picked up Nancy, she lay her head on my shoulder and stuck her thumb in her mouth. "She's a sweet girl," Pam whispered, touching Nancy's dark curls.

"Yes, she is," I replied as I picked up our bag.

"I have a twelve-year-old son. He comes into the diner from time to time," she said. "I am sure you'll meet him soon." She locked the door then turned around. "So I overheard your conversation with Adam. You're new to town?"

"Yes, I arrived just this morning."

"Well, that's very new. Do you have a place to stay?"

"No, I don't. Do you know of a cheap motel around here?"

"Yes, there's one about three blocks south, then take a right, go another block, and you'll see it, the Sunrise Motel. Nothing fancy, but it will serve its purpose."

"Thank you," I replied.

"See you in the morning, Anne. And don't be late . . . Adam is a stickler for time!"

***

The next morning, I worked from 5:30 am until 2 pm. Adam then told me to take a break and come back at five for the dinner shift. I was glad to have the job, but the hours were crazy, and I still needed to find a place for Nancy to stay. As I sat on the beach watching Nancy play along the water's edge, I picked up handfuls of sand, sifting it through my fingers. I looked down at my wedding ring. Tears immediately fell from my eyes. The truth was, despite all his lies, all the anger and betrayal I felt toward him, I still loved Sam. I was so stupid! How did I let this happen to me? How did I not know he was lying to me . . . that he had another family? And the money . . . why? Why did he do it? He made enough for us to get by on his salary. So why did he scam so many people out of their life's savings? Sam said he would never hurt me, and yet here I was with my heart breaking. I had given him everything . . . never again would I trust a man! I wanted to take the ring off, but this ring is what got me the job . . . Adam never would have hired me if he thought I wasn't married when I had Nancy. Of course, the truth was, I wasn't . . . but I hadn't known that, and he didn't need to know the truth. Plus, I guess wearing the ring wasn't so bad. It was Aggie's, and it was the only thing left of hers that I had.

"Nancy! Come along," I called out as I stood and brushed the sand off the back of my dress.

"Mama, Mama, look," she said as she came running over. "Look, Mama, for you."

I took the item she held out to me. It was a shell. A beautiful shell, like nothing I had ever seen before. It was round, shiny, and smooth with brown dots. I held it up to my ear and smiled. I could hear the ocean, a trick Sam had taught me the last time we were here.

"Listen," I said, holding the shell up to Nancy's ear. "Do you hear that?" She nodded. "It's the ocean." She smiled. "Now, no matter where we are, we can always hear the ocean. Come, Nancy, we have to go," I said, taking her hand.

"Aw, Mama," she protested.

"We'll come back another day. I promise," I replied. "Mama is tired, and I want to rest a bit."

"Like your shell, Mama?" she asked as we walked through the sand toward the sidewalk.

"Yes, baby, I love it. I'm going to keep it forever."

***

When we arrived back at the hotel, there was a woman sitting just outside our room smoking a cigarette. "Afternoon," she said. "You the new girl? I heard a new girl was staying here."

"I guess," I replied.

"Sandy," she said, smiling and holding out her other hand.

"Anne," I said, reaching out, shaking her hand.

"It's nice to meet you, Anne." She then looked at Nancy. "Who is this?"

"This is Nancy. Nancy, this is Ms. Sandy."

"Hi, Ms. Sandy," Nancy said shyly.

"No Ms. Just Sandy," Sandy replied. "I ain't no Ms."

I removed the key from my pocket and unlocked the door to our room. Nancy rushed past me, running over to the bed and picking up Dolly. "It was nice to meet you, Sandy," I said as I, too, stepped into the room.

"Hey," she said, following me. "You working somewhere?"

"Yes, I have a job at a diner."

"You off at night?" she asked.

"We close at nine," I replied.

"Perfect."

"Why is that?" I asked, confused.

She took another puff on her cigarette, threw it to the ground just outside my door, then stepped on it, twisting her toe. "I got three kids, and I need someone to watch them for me while I work. The lady who was watching them for me left three days ago. I ain't worked since then, and I need the money." I opened my mouth to speak, but Sandy cut me off. "Please . . . it's easy. You come home, they come over, and they go to bed. They sleep, and I pick them up in the morning at six."

"Sandy, I have to be at work at 5:30 every morning," I said.

"Who's watching Nancy for you?"

"I haven't found a sitter for her yet," I replied.

She smiled. "You watch my kids for me at night, and I'll watch Nancy for you during the day."

"Won't you be sleeping during the day if you're up working all night?" I asked.

"Some," she replied. "But my daughter is ten, and she can help keep an eye on Nancy . . . she helps me with my other two."

I looked over at Nancy. Should I leave her with this strange woman and a ten-year-old? But what choice did I have? I had to keep this job, or we would be out on the streets. Besides, once Nancy and I were more settled, I could find another arrangement for her care if I needed. "Alright, we have a deal," I said.

Sandy smiled.

***

September 1950

Despite my initial fears and concerns, the agreement I had with Sandy worked out well for the both of us. Her daughter Alicia was very mature for her age, and Nancy quickly took to her. Sandy also had a daughter Pearl who was a year older than Nancy and a son David who was six. They were all sweet children, and I had it easy. When I got home from work, all I had to do was tuck them into bed — they had already been bathed and fed. It wasn't long before I realized what kind of work Sandy did. Each night, men would show up at her door, some different, some same. But I didn't judge her. If things hadn't worked out for me the way they had, I might have ended up doing what she was.

I had now been working at the diner for a year. The hours were long, but I didn't complain. I had Sundays off and a job that paid just enough to keep food on the table and a roof over our heads. I enjoyed working with Adam and Pam, and I even got to know several of our loyal customers. Even though life had not turned out how I had imagined, it was going well. Nancy and I were happy, healthy, and getting by on our own.

Coming home for my afternoon break, I noticed boxes of stuff sitting outside Sandy's room. As I neared, I recognized some of the items — they belonged to Sandy. The door to her room was slightly open, so I opened it all the way and stepped inside. Everything was cleaned out, and Sandy and the children weren't there. Immediately my heart began to race. Where was Nancy? Sandy had been watching Nancy for me. As I stepped out, I ran into the cleaning woman.

"Jane, where's Sandy?" I asked.

"She's gone."

"Gone? What do you mean gone? She has my Nancy!"

"I'm sorry. I was just told to clean the room out, and that she was gone. I don't know anything else."

Trying to stay calm, I ran to the motel's office. Perhaps Jeff knew what had happened to Sandy and where Nancy was. When I opened the door and stepped inside, I saw Nancy sitting in a chair with Dolly in hand. I let out a huge sigh of relief.

"Mama!" Nancy called out as I fell to my knees and hugged her tight. "Mama, you're squeezing me!"

Releasing her, I smiled. "I'm sorry, baby. I was just worried about you when I came home, and you weren't in the room."

"Mr. Jeff was watching me, Mama."

I nodded then kissed her forehead. "You go on back to our room. I'll be right there."

I stood by the door and watched Nancy, making sure she went straight to our room without any detours. Once she was safe inside, I walked over to the desk. I wanted to find out what had happened to Sandy. It wasn't like her to just take off, especially without telling me.

"Thanks for watching her, Jeff," I said as I approached the desk.

"No problem," he replied.

"Can you tell me what happened to Sandy?"

"She was kicked out."

"Why?"

"The owners found out what she did for a living, and they made me throw her out."

"But she has children . . . she was only doing what she had to do to survive!"

Jeff shrugged his shoulders. He was a few years younger than me, early twenties, not married and no children of his own, so I figured he didn't understand the struggles of raising a child, especially as a single woman. I knew Jeff was only doing his job making Sandy leave, but still, I felt bad for her. I wondered where she was, and what she was going to do. Then I wondered what I was going to do. I now had to find another sitter for Nancy.

"You don't know of anyone who could watch Nancy for me while I work?" I asked.

"Well, actually, I do," he said. "I might know of someone who would be willing to watch her."

"Really?" I asked hopefully.

He grabbed a piece of paper and wrote something on it before handing it to me. "My sister Erin. That's her address. It's not far from here."

"Thank you," I replied, smiling. "Thank you so much."

"Any time, Anne," he replied as I walked out the door.

***

I was standing in front of a small house about four blocks from the motel. The grass was tall and needed to be cut. The paint was just beginning to peel, and there was junk and trash all over the yard. The place was rough, and it wasn't just this place. It was the entire neighborhood. Looking down at Nancy, I wasn't sure this was the best option, but what other option did I have? I had to be at work in thirty minutes. Hand in hand, we walked down the path to the front door, stepping around toys as we did. At least there were other children here, I thought. I knocked on the door and immediately heard footsteps. Seconds later, the door opened. A young boy answered. He was no more than six or seven. Standing behind him was a little girl who looked to be the about same age as Nancy.

"I'm looking for Erin," I said, smiling.

"Mama," the boy called.

Seconds later, a young woman came walking down the hall toward the door. She looked to be a few years younger than I. She had blonde hair and beautiful green eyes. She was very pretty but looked extremely tired. Then I noticed she was pregnant—very pregnant—which explained the tiredness. I wasn't sure if this was a good idea. Her hands were already full, and she had another on the way. She looked me over but didn't say anything.

"Hi," I said. "My name is Anne. Your brother Jeff sent me here."

"Did he?" she said with an almost sarcastic tone. I nodded. "Go on, Billy," she said. "You too, Susan." The children ran off, and she turned her attention back to me. "So what do you want?"

"Well, I'm looking for someone to watch my daughter while I work, and Jeff gave me your name."

Erin now looked Nancy over. "Does she mind?"

"Yes, she's a good girl," I said.

"What are your hours?"

"I work six days a week, and I'm off on Sundays. Five thirty to two, and then again from five to nine."

"I'll do it for thirty bucks a month."

"Thirty! I can't afford that!" I exclaimed.

"That's my price. Take it or leave it," she said.

I looked down at Nancy. How was I going to afford this? Our motel cost forty dollars a month, and that was a lot for me. Erin was asking a phenomenal amount to watch Nancy, yet if I didn't show up to work, I would lose my job. "Alright, but I can't pay until the end of the week."

"Fine. Come along, Nancy," she said, reaching out her hand. "Your mama has to go to work."

***

November 1950

Two months had passed since Erin began to watch Nancy for me. I had pawned Aggie's ring to cover the cost of childcare. I hated to do it because it was the only thing I had of hers, but I desperately needed the money. In the meantime, I had looked for another who might be willing to watch Nancy for less. There was no one, not when they found out I was a single mother with no husband. I had even tried a local church that I was told had a childcare program, but they, too, turned me away.

I recently received a letter from Sandy letting my know that she and her kids were safe and living in Chicago with her brother. That if I ever needed anything to call. I was glad to know she was alright.

I now stood next to the bed, looking down at my money. After I had paid Erin and bought a few groceries, I had only half of what I owed for the room. Gathering up the money, I looked at Nancy, who was lying on her stomach coloring in her coloring book.

"You stay here. I'll be right back."

"Okay, Mama," she replied as she continued coloring in her book. "Mama, can I watch the television?" she asked right before I stepped out of the room.

"May you . . . may you watch television. And yes, you may," I said.

I saw her sit up and jump off the bed as I closed the door to our room. I walked slowly to the office. I was hoping since they knew me, and never once had I been late on a payment, they would give me a break. The bells rang over the door as I stepped into the office. No one was in, so I walked up to the desk and hit the bell sitting on the counter. I wasn't sure if Jeff or the owner Harold was working, but either way, they both knew me. A few seconds later Jeff appeared through the doorway behind the desk.

"Here to make your payment?" he asked. I nodded and handed him the money. "This isn't enough," he said after he had counted it.

"I know ... it's just ... you see, now that I have to pay for childcare, well, I don't have the entire amount just yet. I was hoping you could give me a few more days."

"How did you pay the last two months?" he asked.

"I sold a ring. I just need a few days, Jeff, and I will get the money."

"Did you get another job?"

"No ..."

"Then what will a few more days do?" he asked.

He was right. How was I going to pay? And I didn't have anything else to sell, nothing worth anything. I needed another job, yet with the hours I was already working, that would be impossible.

"Tell you what," he said. "You come with me. I think we can work this out."

"You have a job for me?" I asked as I walked around the front counter.

"Something like that," he whispered. "In here," he said as he opened the door to the room from which he had just come.

I stepped through the doorway into a small room that held a cot, a table with a chair, and a television. The television was on, and *Sky King* was playing. Hearing the door close behind me, I spun around to find Jeff standing just inches away. Reaching out, he touched my arm then ran his fingers across my neck. The way he looked at me reminded me of Frank. "What are you doing?" I asked nervously.

"Collecting the payment."

I shook my head. "Not this way," I whispered. "I thought that perhaps you had something for me to do."

"What else would you be good for Anne," he said as he pushed me toward the cot.

"Jeff, please."

"Alright ... go," he said, taking a step back. "Pack your bags and leave."

I stood looking at him. "I have nowhere to go."

"That's not my problem. I offered you a way to pay for your room, and you refused . . . unless you've changed your mind."

***

I sat on the edge of the cot, buttoning the front of my dress and trying to hold in my tears the entire time. Once I was buttoned, Jeff held his hand out to me. I didn't want to touch him, but I placed my hand in his, and he pulled me to my feet.

"Same time next week," he said. I didn't answer but just stared at him. He reached out and ran his fingers through a lock of my hair, smiling as he did. "Did you think this was a one-time thing?" I nodded. "If you want a place to stay, then you will meet me here once a week. Otherwise, you can take Nancy and leave . . . understood?"

***

"Mama, I'm hungry," Nancy said as I walked past the bed.

"You'll have to wait," I replied as I shut the bathroom door.

I turned on the water in the tub, plugged the drain, stripped my clothes off, and stepped in. As the tub filled with water, I cried and cried. Then, taking a bar of soap, I scrubbed my body. I felt so dirty and used. I was also angry and disgusted with myself.

"Mama," Nancy said, peeking her head through the doorway. "Are you crying, Mama?"

"No," I lied as I wiped my tears, trying my best to pull myself together.

"Why are you crying, Mama?" she asked.

"I'm just tired. Mama will be okay."

She nodded. "I'm hungry, Mama," she said.

"I'll make dinner as soon as I'm done bathing," I replied. She nodded again. "Go on, Nancy. I'll be out shortly."

She closed the door, and I began to cry again. Why was this happening to me? How did I end up here? And how could I have let Jeff touch me?

NINE

<u>April 1951</u>

I hated sleeping with Jeff. Each time I did, I would return to my room, strip my clothes, and soak in a bath where I would cry and cry. Each time, I felt dirty, used, and disgusted. I felt trapped too. I continued to look for a less expensive caregiver for Nancy and couldn't find one. I even considered taking another job, but the hours I already worked wouldn't allow for it. Things only got worse . . . for I was now pregnant. I hid my pregnancy for as long as I could, but now, at about four months, I was beginning to show. It was 5:20 one Friday morning. I was tired, and my back was hurting, but I had to work, so I opened the door to the diner and walked in. Almost immediately, Adam approached. He stood, looking down at my belly.

"Are you with child? I heard rumors that you might be pregnant."

I would have lied if I could have gotten away with it, but my belly was just going to continue to grow. "Yes," I reluctantly whispered.

"I have to let you go, Anne," he said, making eye contact with me.

"Adam, please," I begged. "I need this job. I can do it, even in my condition."

"I'm sorry, Anne. Your husband isn't here, and you're with child . . . people are talking." Instantly, tears fell from my eyes. He pulled some money from his pocket and handed it to me. "Today's wages. I can't do anything more to help you." I nodded as I took the money and placed it in my pocket. "I'm sorry it didn't work out," he continued. "You're a sweet young lady and a hard worker, but I just can't have you here . . . it's not good for business. You understand." With tears falling, I nodded then turned, making my way to the door. "Good luck, Anne!" he called after me.

***

Two days had passed, and I couldn't find a job anywhere. If I thought finding a job was difficult when I first arrived, well, now it was impossible. No one would dare hire a pregnant woman, especially one with no husband. The afternoon of the second day when Nancy and I arrived back at the hotel, I found all my things sitting outside the door to my room. My heart sank. I got the message—I was no longer welcome there.

"Mama, why is our stuff outside?" Nancy asked.

"Because we're moving," I replied, forcing a smile.

"Where?" she asked.

"Well . . ." What could I say? "Well, it's a surprise," I said as I grabbed my bag, hoping my answer satisfied her. It seemed to have worked because she didn't ask me any more questions.

Living here for the last year and a half, we had accumulated many things, and I had no way to move them, so I packed what I could carry and left everything else on the concrete patio. Nancy was holding her Dolly as well as a few of her favorite books she insisted on taking but I couldn't fit into our bag.

"Come along," I said as I placed my hand on her shoulder and walked toward the office. I had to talk to Jeff. Maybe he could help. After all, this was his child I was carrying. I hadn't told him I was pregnant, though I assumed he knew . . . I had a small belly. "You wait here for me," I said to Nancy as I set our bag on the sidewalk beside her. She nodded, and I stepped inside.

"You can't stay," Harold said as soon as I entered.

"I know . . . I need to talk to Jeff."

"He's not here."

"Do you know where he is?" I asked.

"Nope, he never showed for work. If you see him, you tell him he's fired," Harold said as I left.

***

Erin opened the door, holding her newest baby in her arms. Nancy rushed past her, running inside before I could tell her to stop. I knew she was looking for Billy and Susan. She missed playing with them.

"You working again?" she asked.

"No, I came here to see if you might know where Jeff is."

"He ain't here. Took all my money and left town last night, the bastard." I sighed. Jeff was going to be of no help to me. "Why you looking for him anyway?" she asked. I placed my hands on my dress then pressed down, exposing my belly. "He knocked you up, too, huh? This one is his," she said, looking at her baby. "Billy, too, and he ain't never helped, not one dime. You're better off without him."

"But . . . Jeff, he's your brother!" I said, shocked.

"He ain't my brother," she said, laughing. "We just told people that 'cause he was livin' here for a time . . . and well, you know how things work." I nodded. "You got a place to stay?" she asked, looking down at my suitcase.

"No," I replied. "I don't know what I'm going to do."

"Well, you can stay here for the night," she said stepping back. "Just tonight, then you go your way. I got enough mouths to feed. I don't need to be adding three more."

***

I looked down at the letter I held in my hand, then back up at the building. The address matched. I was standing before a really nice four-story tall brick building on a tree-lined street in a really nice section of the city. *Jeremy must be doing very well for himself*, I thought. "Come along, Nancy," I said, taking her hand.

Hand in hand, we made our way up the steps. Just as we approached, the door opened, and an older woman stepped out. "Good afternoon," she said, smiling when she saw us.

"Good afternoon," Nancy replied. "Mama and I are here to visit my uncle."

"Are you now," the woman said. "And who is your uncle?"

"I don't remember," Nancy replied in a whisper.

The woman looked at me. "Jeremy Smith," I said.

The woman smiled. "I knew Jeremy. He was married to that sweet girl Carol."

"Was?" I asked.

"Well, I'm sure they're still married," she said, smiling again. "But they're not here anymore. Moved out about a month ago. Took a job in Kansas, I believe." I nodded, disappointed. "You didn't know?" she asked. I shook my head. "You did say you were his sister."

"I am. The last letter I received from Jeremy had this as a return address," I replied, holding up the letter.

"I'm sorry. You just missed him." She looked me over then looked at Nancy. "You were coming here for help, weren't you?"

"Yes," I replied.

"Do you have any other family here?"

"No, but I have a friend who lives here in the city. I'll try her next."

"Well, I wish you the best," the woman said as she walked off.

***

Once again, I found myself standing in front of an apartment building. This one was not nearly as nice as the one Jeremy had lived in. In fact, I held my bag and Nancy close as we were in a really rough part of the city.

"Please be home," I said to myself as I knocked on the door. If Sandy wasn't here, I didn't know what I would do. Seconds later, the door opened, and I smiled.

"Anne," Sandy said, throwing her arms around me. "Come in, both of you. What are you doing here?" she asked once we were all standing inside the small apartment.

"I came looking for my brother. He moved, and then I remembered you were living in Chicago," I said as I looked around. The apartment was tiny, old, and sparsely furnished. It was clean, though.

"Where are Alicia, David, and Pearl?" Nancy asked.

Only after she asked did I realize that all three children were gone. "At school," Sandy replied. "They'll be home in about an hour. And they will be very excited to see you." Nancy smiled. "See that door," she asked, pointing.

"Yes," Nancy replied.

"That's their room. You can go play with their toys."

"May I, Mama?" Nancy asked, looking up at me.

"You may," I replied.

"Would you like some coffee?" Sandy asked as Nancy ran off.

"I would love some," I replied.

"So what brought you to Chicago, Anne?" she asked as I followed her into the tiny kitchen. "I mean, aside from your brother?

"I'm pregnant. Lost my job at the diner and got kicked out of the motel."

She nodded as she poured some coffee into two mugs. "Who's the father?"

"Jeff," I whispered as I took a seat at the table. She smiled. "It's not funny, Sandy. He's gone—not that I wanted him, but I don't know what I'm going to do. I don't know how I'm going to make it."

"No, it's not funny," she replied, setting the coffee mugs on the table then sitting. "I was smiling because I don't see Jeff as being your type. How did the two of you end up dating?"

"He's not my type," I replied. "And we weren't dating. After you left, I had to pay for childcare, and I couldn't afford the cost of both the motel and childcare. Sleeping with Jeff kept a roof over my head."

"Well, now you know why I do what I do," she said.

"I never judged you, Sandy," I said after taking a sip of the coffee.

"No, you didn't," she replied. "You were one of the few."

"So are you still . . . are you . . ."

"Yes, I am. Just say it, Anne. I'm a prostitute. You can call me what I am."

"That's not who you are," I replied.

She smiled though I could tell she was holding back tears. "So what are you going to do, Anne?"

"I don't know. I don't have much money, and no one will hire me. Not in my condition."

"You could come work with me," she said.

"I'm pregnant."

"The men don't care. As long as they're getting what they pay for."

I looked down at the coffee mug. "I can't Sandy." I looked back up. "Each time Jeff touched me, I felt dirty and used." I paused and wiped my tears. "I'm ashamed to even talk about it."

She nodded. "You learn to push the feelings away . . . become numb to them."

"I don't doubt it . . . but that's just it," I said. "I don't want to become numb to pain because then I will become numb to joy as well."

A tear fell from each of Sandy's eyes, and she reached out across the table. "You stay here with me until you figure out what you want to do."

"Isn't this your brother's place?" I asked. "What will he say?"

"He ain't here. His job takes him away for weeks at a time. He won't care."

***

May 1951

I stood with Nancy at the end of a very long drive. My feet ached, and my back ached. I ached all over. We had just walked three miles, carrying everything we owned. I was thankful that was all we had walked. At the bus stop in town, we had been offered a ride part of the way. Otherwise Nancy and I would have had to walk about ten miles or so. Thankfully, we were almost at our destination. I could see a huge farmhouse standing at the far end of a half mile long drive. Fields of corn surrounded us. It was short, not quite knee-high right now, but by the end of the season, it would stand tall, well over my head.

"I'm tired, Mama," Nancy said.

"Me too, baby. We're almost there. See that house up ahead? That's where we're going."

Taking her hand once again, we started walking. I had found an ad in a paper, asking for help. Room and board could be negotiated. I had no idea if the job was still available, or if I would even be considered for it due to my situation. I had thought to call ahead, but then I decided to just show up in person, for I had nothing to lose . . . I had already lost everything. I had been living with Sandy for four weeks and could find no job in the city. I spent the last of my money on bus fare to get out here, so if this didn't work out, it would be a very, very long walk back to the small town I had just come from, and even farther to Chicago. I also knew what would happen to me if I went back to Sandy's. Out of options, I would have no choice but to join her and prostitute myself. As we neared the house, I noticed that everything was in pristine condition. The huge farmhouse was a mixture of red brick and yellow siding. It had white trim and green shutters. Potted plants hung from the porch, and there were several flowerbeds in the front yard. A large red barn sat in the back, and it, too, was in excellent condition. Three huge oak trees sat to the left side of the house, providing a great amount of shade. We walked up the steps and onto the front porch where I nervously knocked on the door. As we waited, I looked down at Nancy and smiled. She smiled back. I was about to knock again when I heard footsteps. Seconds later, the door opened. It was a man. A very handsome man with dark brown hair and brown eyes. He was tall, much taller than me. 6'1" . . . 6'2" . . . and he was fit. I could see his muscles as his shirt was not fully buttoned. He was older than me, but still young, early to mid-thirties maybe. He looked at me, then at Nancy. His face showed no emotion, so I couldn't tell what he was thinking. "May I help you?" he asked. Even his voice was handsome.

"Yes, I'm . . . I was . . ." I couldn't speak. I was suddenly nervous. "I'm here about the job that was advertised in the paper," I finally managed.

"Job's been filled," he replied.

"Now Miles, don't you lie," an older woman said as she pushed him out of the way. "You of all people should know better!" Without a word, the man turned and walked away. He clearly didn't like me. The woman looked first at me, then Nancy. She looked to be in her sixties—her hair was brown but had several strands of gray beginning to show. Even though her face had signs of age, she was still beautiful. I could only imagine what a beauty she had once been. "How do you do?" she said, smiling. "My name is Catherine, and you are?"

"I'm Anne, and this is Nancy," I replied.

"Did someone drive you here?" she asked, looking over my shoulder.

"Part of the way," I replied. "Then we walked."

"Walked! From where?"

"Where the roads cross about three miles back," I replied.

"My heavens, you must be tired and hungry! Come in! Please, come in," she said as she ushered the two of us inside.

The house was just as impressive on the inside as it was on the outside. Everything was clean, neat, and tidy, and really fancy too. It reminded me of Aggie's house only on an even grander scale. Walking down a hall, we passed by a large parlor and then a formal dining room before entering a large kitchen. It was old but clean, and I could tell the new appliances had recently been purchased.

"Please, have a seat at the table," Catherine said as she walked over to the refrigerator. I set my bag down then helped Nancy sit as Catherine pulled a plate of tiny sandwiches out of the refrigerator. "These were left over from a church function I held here at the house yesterday," she said as she set the plate down on the table. "I'm glad they won't go to waste . . . not that I was worried. Miles has a big appetite, and I'm sure he would have finished them off before they went bad."

"Miles, is he your son?" I asked as I sat beside Nancy.

"Yes," she replied.

As we ate the sandwiches and drank lemonade, Catherine asked Nancy lots of questions. And Nancy was all too happy to answer.

"Well," Catherine said when we were finished eating. "Let's go talk. I'll get to these dishes later." She stood from the table, and Nancy and I followed suit. "Nancy, I have a job for you," she said, taking Nancy's hand in hers. I followed Catherine and Nancy down the hall then into a room just across the hall from the parlor. I could not believe my eyes—it was a huge library. On all four walls were built in bookshelves, floor to ceiling. And under a large window was a built-in seat topped with cushions and several pillows. I looked with amazement at the books. I never knew one person could own so many books. I could get lost in here.

"Mama, look!"

I turned around to see Nancy sitting on the floor, on a fancy rug. Beside her was a doll-sized table, with a tiny glass tea set sitting on top. A very fancy doll sat in one of the chairs, and she had already placed Dolly in the other chair. "You be careful," I said.

"Yes, Mama," she replied.

"She'll be fine," Catherine said. "That old toy has not been played with in years. I'm just glad it's getting some use." She looked at Nancy. "You stay here and play. I'm going to take your mother into the room just across the hall so we can talk."

"Yes, ma'am," Nancy said. "I'll be good."

I smiled as did Catherine who motioned for me to follow. I next found myself in a beautiful parlor. There were four large windows letting in lots of natural light. And the curtains, they matched the wallpaper exactly and the furniture's upholstery too. The mantel on the fireplace was marble and had a tile surround. A huge light hung from the ceiling above. An oriental rug covered the floor, and there were potted plants all throughout the room. There was even a piano in the corner of the room. I had never seen anything so fancy in my life.

"So you like to read?" I turned around and looked at Catherine. "I saw you looking at the books," she said.

"Yes, I love to read. Other than a library, I have never seen such a collection before."

She smiled. "I enjoy reading too, but it was my late husband who was the avid reader. All those books were his. Please sit," she said, pointing to a fancy sofa. I did, carefully. I had never sat on anything so nice before. "So you came about the job," she said as she too sat.

"Yes, ma'am."

"You're not from around here. You have an accent. Where are you from?"

How did I answer that question . . . where was I from? "I was born in Virginia. I then lived in Alabama for a time and most recently South Carolina."

"So what brings you here to Illinois?"

"My brother . . . he lived in Chicago for a time," I replied.

"He's not there anymore?"

"No, ma'am . . ."

"Please call me Catherine."

"Catherine . . . well, when I arrived about a month ago, I learned he had moved."

"Where have you been staying?" she asked.

"Fortunately, I have a friend who lives in the city. I've been staying with her."

"Why not stay in the city? Surely you could find a job there," she said. "Why come all the way out here?"

"It's not exactly a heathy place to raise a child, at least not where my friend lives," I explained. "And I . . . I . . ." I looked at Catherine, just knowing that a lady who lived in a house so nice was going to ask me to leave the moment she found out I was pregnant. "I'm pregnant," I whispered.

She nodded. "Yes, I can see that. And the father . . . I assume he is gone."

"Yes, ma'am."

"Were you married?"

"No, ma'am," I whispered, ashamed. She nodded again. "I can do the job if you give me a chance, Catherine. My mother died when I was just a young girl, and I was responsible for running the house. I can cook, I can clean, sew, garden . . . I need this," I said, trying to unsuccessfully hold back my tears. "You are my last hope."

"Alright, you're hired."

My mouth dropped. "Did you just say yes?"

"Yes, I did say yes," she replied, smiling. "The job is yours, Anne. Now if you will come with me, I'll show you and Nancy to your rooms," she said, standing. Still in shock, I too stood to my feet. "Oh, and Anne, you are welcome to any book in that library."

***

As I stood in the kitchen peeling potatoes, I was amazed to be here. I had a job and a roof over my head. Not only did I have a room, but Catherine gave Nancy her daughter's old room. And both our rooms were very fancy, just like every other room in this large farmhouse. Though I was glad to have the job, I felt out of place. I definitely did not fit in here. Looking out the window, I smiled. Nancy was in the garden collecting beans with Catherine. I realized how much I had missed living in the country, the fresh air and the open spaces. I was glad Nancy would get to experience the country, at least for however long we were welcome here.

"Look, Mama, look," Nancy said minutes later as she and Catherine entered the kitchen. "I helped pick these beans, and we're gonna eat them for dinner," she said as she placed the bucket on the table.

"Going to eat, Nancy," I corrected. "And you did a great job."

***

We had made roast chicken, mashed potatoes, green beans, and bread for dinner with cookies for dessert. It had been a long time since I had cooked a meal like this as I hadn't a kitchen in the motel in which to do so. The smells that now filled the room brought back memories of my childhood, sitting around the kitchen table with my family. Of course, we never ate this well or off such fine china, but we always ate together. I set the bread basket down on the table just as Miles entered the kitchen through the back door. He looked at me then at Nancy who was already sitting. Then, without a word, he walked over to the sink and washed his hands.

"Please sit, Anne," Catherine said.

I pulled the chair that was next to Nancy and sat, and we all sat quietly, waiting for Miles to join us.

"I see you hired her," he said as he took his place at the head of the table.

"Yes, I hired her. And her name is Anne," Catherine replied.

I could tell Miles was not happy about his mother's decision. He looked at me once again then bowed his head and said grace. It was short and to the point.

"Since you walked here, I assume you will need me to pick you up each morning and drive you home in the evenings," he said gruffly as he began to dish some potatoes onto his plate.

"No, Miles, you won't need to take Anne anywhere," Catherine said. "She and Nancy will be staying here with us."

"What?" he said, his voice slightly raised.

"Now Miles . . . the ad said—"

"I know what the ad said, Mother, and I don't agree with your decision."

"Miles, calm down," she said now, slightly raising her voice. "This is my house, and it's my decision, and I thought it was best for us all to have Anne and her daughter stay here."

He took a deep breath and shoved a few bites of food into his mouth. "Where is she staying?"

"In the guest room, and Nancy is going stay in Elizabeth's room."

"No, I forbid it . . . she can stay with Anne in the guest room."

"Miles Jacob Anderson, what is wrong with you?" she said, voice raised once again.

"It's Elizabeth's room," he said in a stern voice.

"Yes, and she won't be needing it."

We all ate in silence for several minutes. Even Nancy who was usually chatty ate silently. It was quite obvious that Miles did not want me here. I felt awkward. And I hated that I was causing problems.

"This food is delicious Anne," Catherine said, breaking the silence. "Don't you think so Miles?"

"It was alright," he said, standing. "I have some more work to do."

"I'm sorry for his behavior," she said when Miles was gone. "I don't know what has gotten into my son."

"It's alright," I replied. "I'm a stranger and an unwed mother. It's no wonder he doesn't want me here."

She smiled as she reached out, taking my hand in hers. "You are not unwanted, Anne. I want you here."

***

That evening after I put Nancy to sleep, I wandered out to the front porch. I wanted to see the stars. Living in the city, the stars were not as bright at night as they were out here in the country. Just as I thought, the sky was amazing. The heavens were all lit up. Hearing a board creak, I looked to my left. Miles was standing on the porch just a few feet away.

"I'm sorry. I didn't realize you were out here," I said. "I'll go back inside."

"You can stay," he said gruffly.

"I'm sorry that I've upset you," I said a few minutes later, trying to break the awkward silence. "Your mother told me about Elizabeth. I lost my brother Eric in the war . . . I know what it's like to lose someone you love."

"Where was he?" he asked.

"North Africa."

"Never got there . . . I was in the Pacific."

"You fought . . . of course you did," I said. "That was a stupid question."

"Lost a lot of friends in that war," he whispered. We stood silently for several minutes. "Where is Nancy's father?" he asked, breaking the silence.

"Prison," I replied in a whisper.

"How old are you Anne?"

"Twenty-six," I replied. "And you?"

"Twenty-nine."

Once again, we stood silently for several minutes. I was thankful he didn't ask me anything about the child I now carried. He knew I was pregnant . . . it was obvious, and there was no hiding it anymore.

"Well, good night," I said, feeling awkward, then walked back into the house.

TEN

<u>September 1951</u>

The months came and went, and summer turned to fall. Miles kept his distance from me, and I learned why very early on. He was a pastor. Unlike me, he was good. His church was in town, and just like I had when I lived with Aggie, we went to church every Sunday and Wednesday. I didn't mind. I hadn't been to church since Aggie passed, and I figured it was about time I went back. Plus, Nancy enjoyed it. She especially enjoyed Sunday school where she was around other children her age. Though Miles did not like me, he loved Nancy. Which was a good thing because she followed him around everywhere he went. At first, I think it did bother him, but he quickly warmed up. Every once in a while, when I watched Miles with Nancy, I would think of Sam. He had missed so much, and Nancy was missing out on having a father. Sam had written several letters and sent them to my sister Helen, who then forwarded them to me. But I never responded. I didn't even open them. I found out he was sentenced to twenty years, and though he would probably get out earlier, by the time he did, Nancy would be grown. Plus, I didn't want anything to do with a thief and a liar. I was scrubbing the bathroom floor when I felt something strange and warm down below. Looking down, I couldn't see much, for my belly was much too big. Feeling with my hand, I was wet, very wet. I didn't know what had happened, but I was pretty sure I hadn't wet myself. At least I didn't suspect that had happened, but maybe it did. I carefully stood, and shortly after doing so, I felt an intense cramp. I slowly made my way downstairs, then down the long hall into the kitchen where Catherine was rolling out dough with Nancy . . . they were making cookies to sell at the church bake fair. Feeling another cramp, I grabbed my stomach. This one took my breath away. When it was over, Catherine was at my side.

"When did the pains start?"

"Hours ago . . . I think. I haven't been feeling well all day. And just now in the bathroom, something happened. I . . . I . . . I think I might have wet myself," I said, embarrassed.

She smiled. "I bet your water broke. See, I told you to take it easy. Alright, Nancy," she said, "we'll have to finish making these cookies later. I need to help your mama."

"Is the baby coming?" Nancy asked as she and Catherine walked over to the sink.

"It sure is," Catherine replied.

I stood in the doorway, watching as the two began to wash their hands. Their conversation continued, but I was no longer listening as another intense pain had begun. When it was over, I looked up, and Catherine was standing by my side. "Come, let's get you cleaned up and settled into bed. Then I'll call the doctor."

***

"Deep breath," Catherine said in a calm voice. "Breathe . . . good . . . good . . ."

"Mother, are—" Miles said, entering the bedroom as the door was wide open. When he realized what was going on, his face went white. "Oh . . . I'm sorry," he said, quickly turning to leave.

"No . . . you stay here," she called out. "I'll need your help."

"Call the doctor," he protested.

Yes, I thought, *we don't need him here. The doctor will be here soon.* That's what Catherine had told me long ago anyway.

"I already did," she replied. "He's stuck in an emergency surgery."

"Then I'll take her to Chicago . . . they have lots of doctors there."

"Miles, don't be silly…it's too late to take her anywhere. This baby is coming! Plus, we don't need a doctor. I birthed all my babies right here in this house as did my mother."

Feeling another pain come on, I cried out. I don't remember anything else . . . other than Miles stayed at my side the remainder of my labor.

***

"You have a son," Catherine said with joy hours later as she held my son in her arms. I laid my head back on my pillow, relieved that it was all over. I still was not sure how I felt about Miles being in the room while I gave birth. Sam had not even been allowed in the room when I gave birth to Nancy. But regardless, I was relieved, it was over, and my baby was healthy; I could hear his cries. "I need you to take the baby, Miles," she said.

"I don't . . ." Miles started to protest.

"Don't you argue with me, son," she said in a stern voice. Reluctantly, he left my side and took the baby from Catherine who then wrapped him up in a blanket. "You can hold your son in just a few minutes, Anne," she said as she took her position once again. "I have a few more things to do before we're completely finished."

***

Minutes later Miles handed me my son. Tears fell down my face the moment I laid eyes on him. Despite how he came to be, he was perfect.

"He's beautiful," Miles said, smiling at me. I nodded, smiling back. And I was surprised—Miles never smiled . . . not at me anyway. At Nancy and others, yes, but not me. "He has a good set of lungs too."

"Yes, he does," I agreed as I looked back down at my son.

"What will his name be?" Catherine asked, coming to the other side of my bed.

"Ethan, Ethan Eric."

"It's perfect," she said, smiling with tears in her eyes.

"Where's Nancy?" Miles asked.

"She fell asleep a few hours ago," Catherine replied.

"She will be excited to discover she's a big sister when she wakes up in the morning," he said as he touched Ethan's tiny hand. "And she is not going to want to go to school tomorrow either."

"Yes, she will be excited, and I suppose missing a day of school won't do her any harm," Catherine said. "As long as you're in agreement," she said, looking at me." I nodded, knowing there was no way I was going to convince Nancy to go to school in the morning, not with her new baby brother here. Besides, Catherine was correct, missing a day of kindergarten wasn't going to do her any harm.

"Pretty amazing birthday gift," Miles said.

I had forgotten all about that! Nancy's birthday was on Saturday, just two days from now. We had planned a big birthday party, invited all her new friends from school as well as many families from church. We had games planned, and food, and pony rides . . .

"What are we going to do now?" I said. "What about the party?"

"Don't you worry about a thing," Catherine said. "You just rest. Miles and I will take care of everything, won't we, Miles?"

"Of course," he replied. "We can't cancel Nancy's party. It would break her little heart."

I nodded, holding in my tears as I did. "Thank you. I don't know what I would do without you, the both of you," I said, looking between the two. "Thank you for everything."

"You don't need to thank us, dear," Catherine replied. "We're glad to help. Truth is, you and your little ones are just as much a blessing to us as we are to you. Now out with you, Miles," Catherine said, shooing him away. "This baby needs to eat."

Miles smiled at me once again as he stood to his feet. As soon as he left the room and the door closed behind him, Catherine began to unbutton the front of my blouse. "What are you doing?" I asked, feeling slightly violated.

"Just getting you ready to nurse."

"Oh no," I said. "Formula . . . he needs formula. That's what they gave Nancy in the hospital. They told me it was better."

"Rubbish," she said. "You mean to tell me that a man-made substance is better than something God created? No, you will nurse this baby." She then helped position Ethan onto my breast. It felt strange yet at the same time so fulfilling. "There," she said as he was making suckling noises. "Look at that! See, he knows just what to do."

I looked down at Ethan, still in awe of him. Then I had a thought . . . who was he? I mean, yes, he was my son, but what was his last name? I didn't even know Jeff's last name. Instantly, tears began to fall.

"What's wrong, sweetie?" Catherine asked.

"I . . . I . . ." I wiped my tears before I continued to speak. "I don't know his father's last name . . . I don't know what Ethan's last name is."

"Give him your last name, Anne," she replied, smiling compassionately.

My last name, I thought. *Who was I? Was I Anne Mathis, Anne Jones, or Anne Smith? I don't even know who I am.* Then I had a thought. "May I give him your last name, Catherine? After all, you're the one who delivered him."

"Oh, Anne, you are the one who did all the hard work."

"But I couldn't have done it without you," I replied. "Besides, Ethan Eric Anderson does sound good."

Catherine smiled again. "I like it too, though I am not sure legally if you can do that as I have no blood ties to this child. However, I will call my late husband's business partner in the morning and see what we can do."

I nodded, smiling. "How many children did you have, Catherine?" I asked.

"Why do you ask?"

"Well . . . I . . . the way you told Miles about birthing babies at home . . . well, it sounded like you have had several children, more than just Miles and Elizabeth." She sat quietly for several seconds, and I wondered if I had spoken out of place. "I'm sorry I asked," I whispered.

Sitting on the bed beside me, Catherine placed her hand on my leg. "I have five children. I lost the first two before they were even born. My third died just three weeks after he was born. Tommy, he was frail little thing." A tear ran down her face. "Miles and Elizabeth were my only two that survived. Miles was strong from the day he was born. Strong and stubborn like his father. And ten pounds . . . try birthing that." She paused, smiling, "It wasn't easy, I tell you." I, too, smiled. "Elizabeth, well . . . she was born weak like Tommy. Doctors told me she would die within the first few weeks just like her brother. But she didn't—she lived. And she grew . . . and despite her weakness, she was so joyful. A friend to everyone, and in turn she was loved by everyone who ever met her. She was fifteen when the Lord took her home. She died peacefully in her sleep. It was hard on all of us, but it was especially hard on Miles. He adored her. He had watched over her from the day she was born." Tears were now pouring down both of our faces. Catherine patted my leg and smiled. "I will see her again. I will see them all, my husband included."

"Do you really believe that?" I asked. "That we will see our loved ones again?"

"If they accepted Jesus as their savior, then yes, I know we will see them."

"Your babies didn't accept Jesus," I said. "They never had a chance."

"No, but our God is a loving God, Anne," she said. "And he has an exception to that rule. All babies go to heaven. It's not until you reach the age of accountability that you are held responsible for your destination when you leave this world."

"If God is so good, then why did he take your children from you?"

"God does not cause bad things to happen," she explained. "We live in a fallen world full of sin. He didn't want me to lose my children, but he will use it for his glory. And someday, when I get to heaven, I will understand why he allowed it. Until then, I have to trust and have faith. He loves me, and he loves you, and he loves this little guy," she said as she gently rubbed Ethan's head. There was a knock on the door. "Come in," she called out. A second later, the door opened, and a young man not much older than me entered the room. "Doctor Blithe. You finally made it."

"Sorry I'm so late, Catherine," he said, walking over to my bedside. "It's been a long day." Ethan was still nursing, and I felt odd. "How are you feeling?" he asked me.

"Fine," I replied shyly.

"And what's your name," he asked as he set his bag down then pulled a chair over next to the bed.

"Anne," I whispered.

He reached out and gently picked up Ethan's little arm. "How was the birth?"

"She did wonderful," Catherine said. "And everything went well. Turns out we didn't need you after all. You had better watch out . . . I just might run you out of a job."

He smiled at Catherine, then looked back at me. "Well, when little man is done feeding, I'll examine you both, and we shall see just how good a doctor Ms. Catherine actually is."

***

"Ethan is doing very well," Dr. Blithe said. "How are you feeling?"

"Good," I replied.

It had been three weeks since Ethan was born, and Catherine had driven me into town for his first checkup. "Getting plenty of rest and drinking lots of water?"

"Yes."

"And you're still nursing him?" I nodded. "And by the looks of him, I assume that's going well?"

"Yes, Catherine insisted I nurse instead of using formula."

"Well although most of my fellow physicians don't agree, I also think nursing is the best. So if all is going well, then I agree with Catherine."

He looked down, writing something in his chart. When he looked back up, he didn't say anything, just looked at me for several seconds.

"Is something wrong?" I asked.

"Well, no…you see this says you were born in Virginia." I nodded. "Well, it's your name . . . I mean, it's common Smith. And this is going to sound strange, but you look a lot like someone I know. Do you by chance know a Jeremy Smith? He too was originally from Virginia."

"I have a brother named Jeremy," I said. "He's a doctor as well. Married to a woman named . . ."

"Carol," we both said at the same time.

Then we both chuckled. "I went to school with Jeremy," he said. "I'm a few years older, but we were in the same class. I got delayed when the war started and only continued my schooling after I returned home. We both took interns in Chicago. I got hired on here, and he moved to Kansas. I haven't talked to him in a while. How is he doing?"

"To be honest, I don't know," I replied as I tucked a loose strand of hair behind my ear. "I haven't written to him or received a letter in several months. Unfortunately, we're just not that close."

He nodded. "Well, the next time you do talk to him, tell him hello for me."

"I will do that," I said. "Is that all then?"

"Yes, everything looks good. I'll see you and little man again next month."

***

April 1952

It was an abnormally warm April day, so Catherine and I were sitting in the yard on a blanket with Ethan, getting some fresh air. He was seven months old now, crawling and sitting up. He was happily playing with a rattle and some blocks at the moment. The sun and fresh air was a welcome change after having been cooped up indoors most of the winter and early spring. Nancy was at school, and Miles had gone into town to pick up some parts he had ordered for his tractor, so it was just the three of us. "So, Anne," Catherine said, "tell me your story."

I looked at her, wondering why she suddenly wanted to know after all this time. "Why?" I asked, frightened.

"Because I'm curious as to how a beautiful, smart young woman like yourself ended up on my doorstep."

"You took out an ad in the paper, and I answered it."

She took my hand and gave it a gentle squeeze. "Anne, I did not turn you away when you showed up on my doorstep unwed with one child and another on the way . . . what makes you think I will turn you away now?"

I looked down at the blanket we were sitting on and ran my fingers over a small hole.

***

When I finished my story, Catherine sat with tears falling from her eyes, and I saw no judgment, only love. "My dear child," she said, pulling me close. "I thank God that he brought you to me. You and the children."

"How?" I said. "How can you love a God who took away your children and your husband? And look at what he did to me."

"Oh, but don't you see, Anne? God has been walking beside you your entire life. You got away from Frank, and he sent Aggie to you. Even used Sam for a time, and now you are here. Miles and I are your family now. Your forever family. You can stay with us for as long as you wish. You will never again be without a family who loves you or a roof over your head."

"Miles hates me," I whispered.

"Miles can be stubborn, like his father," she said. "But he doesn't hate you, and he adores your children just as I do. Give your heart to Jesus, Anne . . . let him heal all your wounds." I shook my head. "Please, Anne, don't be stubborn. Don't hold on to your hate and your pain . . . it will only be you who suffers—first on this earth and then for eternity—if you choose not to accept God's gift of salvation."

"My brother Eric professed to love Jesus in the last letter he sent me. The same day I received his letter, my father received a letter too. A letter telling him that Eric had been killed. Tell me, Catherine, why God took Eric? Eric gave his heart to Jesus, and then he was killed!"

"Anne, I can't tell you why God called him home. But I can tell you that he's with Jesus, and if you give your life to Jesus, you will see him again. You will see your brother Eric and the child you lost. And you will see Aggie too. This life is temporary. Our real home is with Jesus, and it lasts forever. None of them are dead. Maybe to us here on earth, yes. But our spirit and our souls are eternal."

I sat silently, thinking for several minutes. Catherine, too, was silent. "Even if I wanted to accept this Jesus . . . I don't know how," I said, breaking the silence.

"Well, Anne, that's the easy part," she replied, smiling.

***

August 1952

That spring day in April of 1952 is when I gave my heart to the Lord. I don't have a story of a magical transformation. I was still a single unwed mother. I still struggled with my identity, seeing myself as Christ did. I still struggled to forgive those who had hurt me in the past. But one thing did change that day. I had a peace about me, a peace that filled me, a peace I did not fully understand. I had peace knowing that I had a heavenly father who, unlike my father on this earth, was perfect and loved me with his perfect love. Loved me so much that he could not stand the idea of being separated from me for eternity, so he sent His only son to earth. A man who had no sin and yet was sentenced to death, beaten, hung on a cross, and then died to pay for my sins. A death he did not deserve, yet Jesus went to that cross and was crucified so that I could have life. Not just for eternity, but life here on earth as well. He would never leave me, never forsake me. I knew that no matter what I faced in my future, I would not face it alone. And I knew that someday I would see Eric and Aggie once again . . . that I would meet the child I never got to hold in my arms. A few days later, Catherine gave me a Bible of my very own, and for the first time in my life, I read the word of God. At first, it was difficult, and I didn't understand much. But with Catherine's help and the more time I spent in the word, the clearer everything became. I developed a hunger, a thirst for the word. Now when I participated in church, I no longer did so because it was the "thing to do." I did so because I wanted to help others, to be a blessing to others. I wanted others to experience God's love just as I had. Now as I looked at the world around me, I could see God everywhere. In his creation, in every tree, flower, and animal. When I looked at my children, I was amazed at God's grace and love for me. Despite my shortcomings, he chose to bless me with the two most beautiful children in the world. It was Sunday, and I was sitting between Nancy and Catherine on the first pew, listening as Miles preached. He lit up when he was talking about God. He was excited, and you could see that he truly loved God. Catherine told me that before the war, Miles had gone to school to study law like his father. Of course, he never finished, the war started, and he was sent overseas. When he came back, he had changed and told his mother he was going to be a preacher. She supported his decision, so instead of continuing on at law school, he went off to seminary. When he graduated in 1949, he was hired on here at the local church because their longtime pastor was wanting to retire. The old pastor still preached on occasion to give Miles a break once in a while, but this was Miles's church now, and it was where he was meant to be.

"Anne."

I looked up at Catherine who was standing before me. I then noticed that Nancy was gone . . . church was over, and everyone had been dismissed.

"Come help me set out the food, Anne," she said as I stood. "Then you can go and retrieve Ethan from the nursery."

I followed Catherine out of the sanctuary. It was slow going as we stopped and spoke with several others as we made our way down the aisle. Finally, we made it to the kitchen where plates of food covered every available space on the countertops. We were having a church picnic today, and almost every family had brought something to share. Some even brought multiple dishes . . . we would have plenty to eat. Four other women entered the kitchen just behind us. We each picked up a dish and made our way outside where picnic tables and card tables had been set up under the large sycamore trees. Catherine and the women were all talking, so I just followed silently, lost in thought.

"That was an excellent sermon today," Catherine said as the two of us were making our way back toward the church to collect more food. I nodded. Catherine continued speaking, but I wasn't paying her much attention—my attention was elsewhere. "You alright, Anne," she asked, stopping just before we entered the building. "You're very quiet."

"Yes, I'm fine," I replied, looking over her shoulder at Miles who was standing several feet away talking to the new family that had recently joined our congregation.

Catherine looked over her shoulder then back at me. "You are in love with my son."

"What . . . no . . ." I said, suddenly snapping out of my thoughts.

She smiled. "I don't know how I didn't see it sooner."

"I am not . . . I . . ." I stopped talking, for she was correct. I was in love with Miles. "I . . . I'm sorry."

"Oh, Anne," she said, laughing. "You have nothing to be sorry about. I know I'm partial because he's my son, but he is a wonderful man. Loving him is not a bad thing."

"Except that he doesn't love me," I whispered. "Oh, Catherine, please . . . you can't tell him that I have these feelings for him!"

"I will try my best not to meddle, Anne," she said, still smiling as she patted my arm. "But I wouldn't be at all surprised if my son does have similar feelings for you. Come, let's get the rest of the food put out."

***

September 1952

"There," Miles said as he climbed down the ladder.

"Can I swing? I mean, may I," Nancy asked as she jumped up and down excitedly.

"It's all yours," Miles said as he moved the ladder out of the way.

Nancy immediately sat on the swing, and Ethan followed her as he had just started to walk. He grabbed one of the ropes on the swing and held tight. "Mama, I can't swing with Ethan hanging on!"

"Come here, you," I said, scooping Ethan up into my arms.

"Watch this! I'm going to show you how high I can swing." Nancy began to pump her little legs. "Just like I do on the playground at school."

She went higher and higher until she was squealing with delight. Hearing a car coming up the gravel drive, I turned my head to see who was coming. It was Dr. Blithe's vehicle.

"Is Mother ill?" Miles asked.

"Not that I know of," I replied. "She was just fine this morning."

We both watched as Matt stopped the car and stepped out. When he saw us out in the yard, he started our direction.

"Matt," Miles said, holding out his hand.

"Miles," Matt replied as the two shook.

"Did my mother call you?"

"No," Matt replied. "I'm actually here to see you, Anne. May I have a moment?"

"Sure," I replied.

"Here, let me take Ethan," Miles said, reaching out.

Ethan eagerly went to him, as he always did. I then followed Matt as he began to walk. I followed him over to the fence that separated the yard from the pasture. The horses were grazing just feet away, so I stepped onto the bottom rail of the fence. Betsie, my favorite horse, came over to see if I had a treat.

"Sorry, girl, I don't have anything for you," I said, giving her a pet. Disappointed that I had nothing for her, she walked away to join the others once again. "So what did you want to talk to me about?" I asked.

"Well, I was wondering if you would like to go out with me this Saturday."

"Like a date?" I asked, surprised, as I stepped down off the fence.

"Well, yes," Matt said, smiling. "That's what I was hoping."

"I don't think it would be a good idea," I said.

"May I ask why?"

"You are a doctor, and people in town respect you. I am a single mom with two children from two different fathers. I know what people think about me. What they say about me behind my back. It doesn't bother me like it once did, I'm used to it. But . . . it wouldn't be fair to you. Matt, if you took me out, people would talk. It's a small town."

"I've thought about that, what people might think or say," he said. "And I came to the conclusion that I don't care, Anne. I don't care what others think. You are a beautiful and smart woman, and you're fun to be around. So if you don't have any further objections, I would like to take you out Saturday."

"You know you could have just picked up the phone and called. Saved a trip all the way out here."

"So is that a yes?" he asked, smiling.

***

Matt opened the door for me, and I stepped out of his car. "I had a good time," he said as he walked me up the path toward the house.

"Me too," I replied. "Thank you. It was nice getting out without the children."

"We should do it again . . . soon."

"Perhaps," I replied.

"Is that a yes or a no?" he asked.

"It's neither."

The truth was, I had fun, but Matt was not for me. Sure, he was good-looking, made good money, and he was kind, but there were two things going against him. The first was that he did not have a relationship with the Lord, and I knew I did not want to be unequally yoked with anyone. And the second, well, I was in love with another. Sure, it was a man who did not love me . . . but still, I couldn't betray my heart. As we approached the steps, we both noticed Miles sitting on the porch swing, silently watching us.

"Well, I guess this is good night," Matt said.

"Yes, good night," I replied. "And thank you again."

"No problem. I'll call you soon. See you later, Miles," he said.

Miles nodded, then Matt turned and walked back to his car. "Are the children asleep?" I asked as I made my way up the steps onto the front porch.

"Yes, they went down two hours ago," Miles replied.

"Well thank you for helping watch them tonight. I really appreciate it."

He nodded, and I started for the front door. "Come sit with me," he said just as I reached for the doorknob. I turned around and saw Matt's car slowly driving down the long lane. I then looked at Miles who was still sitting on the porch swing, silently watching me. Slowly, I approached and sat, leaving as much space between us as I could. I wasn't sure what to think. Ever since Ethan was born, Miles had been kinder to me. He would speak to me, but he never sought my attention. "Did you have a good time tonight," he asked a minute or two after I sat.

"Yes."

"Are you going to see Matt again?"

I looked at him, wondering why he cared what I did, who I dated. "No," I replied.

"May I ask why?"

"He's just not for me," I replied. Miles nodded, and we sat silently for several minutes. This was awkward. "Well, I should be getting to bed myself," I said, standing and then taking a few steps toward the front door.

"Marry me, Anne." I stopped in my tracks and spun around. Miles stood from the swing, took one large step toward me, then took my hand in his. "I love you, Anne, and I love your children. And I know I haven't been the kindest to you . . . but you see, God has been working on me. When you showed up on our doorstep, all I saw was a single woman with a child and another on the way. And I will admit, I thought the worst of you. I did not want you here. I did not want anything to do with you. I thought I was better than you. But I was wrong . . . I was so wrong. I am a pastor, and instead of showing you compassion and love . . . I shunned you. I'm no better than the Pharisees in Jesus' time. You are an amazing woman and an even better mother. When you went out tonight, I realized that someone soon is going to come along and sweep you off your feet. I can't lose you, Anne, you or the children. Let me love you. Let me be a father to Nancy and Ethan. Please say yes."

Tears were falling from my eyes. I could not believe my ears. The man I loved was in love with me? No . . . it was one thing for me to love him, but for Miles to love me . . . "I can't marry you, Miles," I said, pulling my hand from his. "You don't know my past, the things I did. I'm not good enough for you. You are good, you are a pastor. I could never be a pastor's wife."

He dropped to his knees and took my hands in his once again. "But you see, I do know your past. Mother told me while you were away tonight. And Anne, I love you all the more. You are not your past. You are a daughter of God, a new creation, and your sins are gone. Cast as far as the east is from the west. And as far as I go . . . I may be a pastor, but I'm human. I'm not perfect. I am far from perfect. I have my own past. Years ago, I ran from God and lived for myself. Someday I'll tell you all about it. And I'm not good—no one is. Only God is good. God has his hand on us . . . I had been praying for a wife for some time when you showed up, and God answered my prayer by bringing you right to my doorstep. But I was too proud, too stupid to realize it at the time. You see, that advertisement for help on the farm, it wasn't for my mother. She didn't want or need help in the house. It was for me. I needed the help. I didn't have enough time to run the farm and minister to the congregation."

"I am so stupid," I whispered.

How did I not realize that? I should have known when Miles hired Isaac just days after I arrived. He smiled. "You're not stupid, Anne . . . the ad mother put out was not very clear. And when she met you and Nancy, she didn't have the heart to send you away, and I'm glad. I need you, Anne. I want you to be my partner in this life. I want to have a family with you. To raise our children here on this farm where I grew up. Then someday, when we're old, gray, and wrinkled, I want to sit on this porch swing with you and watch our grandchildren play in the yard. And then, years later, and God willing, our great-grandchildren. So, Anne, what do you say? Will you be my wife? Will you let me love you?"

Of course, you already know what happened. I said yes, and a month later in October of 1952, Miles and I became husband and wife. We had the church wedding I had always wanted, white dress and all. Almost the entire town showed up to witness our vows. I got to see even more of the world as we honeymooned in Europe while Catherine watched the children for us. We even visited some of the places Eric and Jeremy had been. Just as Miles wanted, we raised our family in this old farmhouse. Catherine lived long enough to see all her grandchildren come into this world. She was by my side for each one of their births, and aside from Nancy, all of my children were born right here in this house. I had my happily ever after. Sure, our marriage had ups and downs. It wasn't perfect—we're both human. Still, Miles was my best friend, my true love. And he did love me. He loved me as much as any man could love a woman. Every day I had with him on this earth was a gift from God.

EPILOGUE

June 2016

My children sat quietly. No one spoke, and there was not a dry eye in the room. They now all knew my story. They knew my mistakes, that Nancy and Ethan were not biologically Miles's children, something neither Miles nor I had ever told them. Mostly because he was their father ... the only father they knew. My children now knew my story ... and they did not judge me. They just asked questions, and I answered them as best as I could. When I was finished, I could tell they all were glad to know the truth, and I too felt better, like a weight had been lifted off my shoulders.

"Are you hungry, Mama?" Nancy asked, looking at the clock when we had finished our discussion. I too looked over at the clock. It was now just after six. "I can heat some of the leftovers up for dinner if you'd like, and we can all stay and eat dinner with you."

"Yes, that sounds good," I replied. "But I think I want to take a walk while you're getting everything ready."

"May I join you, Grandma?" Eva asked as I stood to my feet.

I smiled at her as I patted her arm. "Maybe next time, dear. I just want to be alone for a while."

"Okay, Grandma," she replied. "I'll help Aunt Nancy in the kitchen, then I'll come get you when dinner is ready."

"Sounds good," I said. I watched as she left, following Nancy into the kitchen. Eva was my youngest grandchild, Charlie's daughter. She was twenty-three and engaged to be married soon. Out of all my grandchildren, she was the most like me. I took another look around the room at the rest of my children. How blessed I was. None of them were rich by the world's standards, but each one of my children, their wives, and almost all my grandchildren loved the Lord, and that was priceless. I picked up my tin box from the side table next to Miles's chair then stepped outside through the sliding glass door. I slowly made my way through the yard toward the small cemetery on the property. It took me a lot longer to walk than it had when I was younger, but eventually I made it. I passed under the small metal arch and looked around. The grave markers of Miles's great-grandparents were the oldest. His grandparents were buried here as well. Catherine, her husband, Elizabeth, and her other children were also laid to rest here in this family cemetery. There were twelve markers altogether. The others were children that had been lost to Miles's grandparents and great-grandparents. And the newest marker with a pile of black dirt before it belonged to Miles. I, too, would be buried here someday, right beside him. I approached Miles's grave and slowly sat. I sat, not knowing how I was going to get back up, but I didn't really care either.

"I told them," I said, setting the tin box on the dirt in front of me. "I told our children my story. I miss you, Miles . . . where did the years go? How fast they flew by. It seems like just yesterday I was standing on your doorstep, and Nancy was just a little girl, and Ethan . . . he wasn't even born yet. Oh, Miles, the Bible talks about death's sting being taken away. But it hurts . . . and I miss you so very much. I can't wait to see you again."

"Then come home." I looked up to see Miles standing before me. He was young and so very handsome. Even better looking than I remembered. Smiling, he held out his hands to me. "Come home, Anne, because I miss you too."

I reached out and took his hands. Instantly, I felt this amazing surge of energy throughout my entire being. I looked down, and I saw my body lying on his grave. I looked at my arms and my hands . . . I was young again. "I'm young," I said, looking up at Miles. He nodded still smiling. "Did I die?"

"Well, you're here, aren't you?" he replied. "Your old body is gone, but you're not dead, Anne. You know that. We don't die. We are eternal beings. And this is just the beginning of all eternity. Come," he said. "Come see."

It was then that I realized I was standing in a large field filled with flowers. The colors were so brilliant, and the smells were amazing. All my senses were in overdrive, and yet it was not overwhelming. It was amazing! I looked back down at my body. I had no aches or pains anywhere. And I was clothed in white, pure white . . . a white so bright and so clean. A shade of white I had never seen before. And the peace I felt . . . the indescribable peace. I then looked up toward the sky. There was no sun, no moon, and the sky itself was not blue, but light and bright, full of colors, and it was huge . . . much larger than one could even imagine. Looking back down and to my left, I saw a forest not too far from where we were standing. I saw many varieties of trees that I recognized, and even more I had never seen before. And the colors, how can one describe colors you've never seen? Everything around me was alive . . . I mean, really alive. Everything, the plants and the sky . . . all of creation, it was speaking . . . no, more like singing. All of God's creation was praising him, each in its own way and yet melodically it all made sense, coming together like one amazing symphony. I reached out to touch a flower only to discover it was a butterfly . . . several dozen of them actually. They took flight, swirling all around me for a second before flying away. And they, too, sang.

"They can speak," I said excitedly, spinning around to face Miles.

"Yes, they can . . . all the animals here can speak," he replied. "I guess C. S. Lewis was on to something." I smiled. "Race you to the river," he said.

"The river?" I asked, looking around and not seeing a river anywhere.

"Straight ahead, Anne. You can't miss it," he replied as he took off running. I ran after him. And it was then I realized I was barefoot. But it didn't matter because the ground was so soft. Not only was it soft, but I just knew that nothing here could harm me. I would not fall, I could not be injured, and I would never be sick. And I was running fast, very fast. So fast that in my old body, even in my prime, running like this would have been impossible. A city was now coming into view . . . a huge city. So I slowed down and eventually stopped running altogether. It was then I noticed I wasn't even out of breath. It was as if I had not been running at all. The strength and energy I had was amazing! The city was bright, shining brilliantly, and rose up so tall that many of the structures went high, high up into the heavens. So high I couldn't even see an end to them. And the architecture, well, that too amazed me. It made earthly creations like Versailles seem like nothing more than a cardboard box. The structures were made of pure gold, so pure it was like glass. And there was a rainbow in the sky above the city, the most magnificent rainbow I had ever seen, and the wall . . . the city was surrounded by a wall made of jasper . . . and the foundation of the wall was covered in beautiful stones. I could see three gates from where I stood. They were all open, and each was made from pearl, a single pearl . . . just like the Bible described. Then I saw magnificent creatures standing guard by the gates. Winged creatures, tall, strong, powerful, and beautiful. Angels . . . they were angels. Coming out from each of the three gates along the wall facing this direction was a road, a road paved in gold. It was a gold so pure, and just like the city, it was like clear glass. I then noticed the river. A huge river that flowed right out from under the city's wall. It was the largest, most beautiful river I had ever seen, and its water was crystal clear. Surrounding the river were parks, big beautiful parks filled with trees, plants, and flowers. There was even a gold bridge that crossed the river. And then, for the first time, I noticed other people besides Miles and me. They were standing not too far from the bridge.

"Well, go on, Anne," he said. "There are others here who have been waiting to see you."

"But I just got you back," I said, looking at him.

"Oh, Anne," he said, chuckling as he reached out and stroked my cheek. "I'm not going anywhere. We have all eternity together."

Leaving his side, I began making my way toward the others. A young woman stepped out from the crowd, and I immediately knew who she was . . . it was my mother. "Mama," I said as I wrapped my arms around her. "Oh, Mama, how I missed you!"

"Oh, my sweet Anne," she said, squeezing me tight. "I know you did. But you're here now, and we will never be apart ever again." She held me at arm's length. "Look at you. You're even more beautiful than I remembered."

"I told you she was beautiful." I spun around to see Aggie standing behind me. A young Aggie, but I knew it was her. She didn't have to say, I just knew, just as I knew my mother. There was a young man standing beside Aggie, and I knew, too, who he was even though I had never met him before. It was George, her George. "And where is my hug?" Aggie asked, smiling.

Smiling back, I threw my arms around her. Feeling a tap on my shoulder sometime later (and I say sometime because the thing is, there was no time anymore, at least not like there was on earth), I turned around. "Eric," I said, smiling as we embraced.

"It's about time you showed up," he said, teasing.

"Oh, Eric, how I missed you!"

"Well, that's the funny thing," he explained. "Though I believe you did miss me, I haven't been here all that long, not long before you arrived. Things work differently here than they do on earth."

"Well, I went years without you," I said. "Seventy-three years without you."

"But you're here now," he replied, smiling. "And that's all that matters, Anne. I'm so glad you accepted Christ as your savior. Now we have all of eternity to catch up."

"I am too," I replied.

"Anne." I sucked in my breath. I knew who it was even before I turned around.

It was sweet precious Lillian. Without another word, we embraced. We didn't say anything. There was no need to. The past was gone, it was over, and we were together, never to be hurt or separated again. When I released Lillian, I looked back at Mama and Eric. "Jeremy," I whispered . . . not seeing him anywhere. He had passed away five years earlier.

The moment I said his name, this overwhelming sensation of darkness rushed through me. It happened only for a split second, and then it was gone. But it was a horrid feeling, a feeling completely devoid of God. I then thought of my papa, and the same thing occurred. And I knew at that moment that neither of them were here. I did not rejoice, but at the same time, I was not upset. I knew why they weren't with us. They had not accepted Christ as their savior. They had made their choice as to where they were going to spend eternity, and I fully understood and accepted it.

"Well, you wasted no time following Miles here."

It was Catherine. Once again, I smiled as the two of us embraced. I noticed a young man, and right away I knew he was Miles's father, Jacob. "Anne," he said, hugging me as well. "It's nice to finally meet you. I am so glad God gave you to Miles. That you had each other to do life with. And I can't wait to meet all my beautiful grandchildren."

"I'm glad I had Miles as well," I replied, smiling. "And you will . . . you will get to meet all your grandchildren, and many of your great-grandchildren as well." I then saw Miles standing under a tree, speaking with two young men and a woman. "Those are your—"

"Yes," Catherine said, cutting me off. "My children. I told you I would see them again."

I noticed a young man standing by Lillian, and I knew it was her son, the son who had died along with her. I just knew who people were even if I had never met them before. I knew them, just as they knew who I was. A small boy came running over, no more than six or seven. He ran right up to me and threw his arms around me. Instantly I knew who he was . . . he was my great-grandson Jacob, named after both his great-grandfather and grandfather. Six years earlier, Charlie's eldest daughter Melissa had Jacob, but he was born with a heart defect and died just two weeks after he was born. I dropped to my knees, and I looked him over . . . he was beautiful. "Is Mama coming soon?" he asked.

"Yes," I replied. "She will be here before you know it."

It wasn't a lie. Just like Eric said, things were different here . . . before long, all my loved ones would be here. "That's what great-grandpa Miles told me," he said smiling. "Jesus too. He said Mama would be coming soon. I'm glad you're here great-grandma, and I can't wait to see my mama."

"And your mama, she can't wait to see you," I replied, hugging him once again.

"Well, I am going to go play now," Jacob said when I released him.

I stood, smiling and watching as he ran off to join a large group of young children.

"You look just like I remember."

I knew that voice, and I was shocked to hear it. Surprised, I turned around to see Sam standing behind me. "You're here!" I said excitedly.

"I am, by the grace of God. You see, the whole prison thing, though I was not so excited about it on earth, well, God knew what I needed. I didn't have much to do locked up hours upon hours a day. I found a Bible a few years after I had been incarcerated. Started reading it only because I was bored, but eventually things changed. I read the gospel story, and for the first time in my life, it became clear. I understood it, and I could no longer ignore it. So here I am."

I smiled, so very glad to see him. I had absolutely no ill feelings toward him, none whatsoever . . . only love. Though the love I felt for him was a different love than I had ever felt on earth. Even my feelings for Miles were different now. Oh, I loved Miles deeply. I always would. But we were no longer married, not here. And it didn't bother me like I used to think it would. Here, I didn't need our marriage relationship, not like I did on earth. I also knew that Sam had no ill feelings toward me. He had tried to keep in contact over the years, but I didn't allow it, and I kept Nancy from him. None of that mattered now. All the mistakes I had made on earth, they did not matter. It was all washed away. In fact, the only reoccurring idea that kept coming into my mind since I had first arrived was, *Did you love Jesus, and did you love others?*

"Nancy . . . she's beautiful," I said. "She was such a good child, so kind and talented, so very talented. She is an amazing artist. Oh, and she has three boys, and they, too, have children. And she loves the Lord. You will see her again."

"Yes, I know," he said, smiling. "And I'm looking forward to that day."

"How do you know Nancy will be joining us?"

"Just think of a loved one on earth," he replied. I thought of my granddaughter Eva, and instantly a feeling of overwhelming peace came over me . . . I knew she belonged to Christ. Of course, I knew that while I was on earth, but this knowing was different. "Pretty cool isn't it?" he said, smiling. I nodded, and then I looked around. I was surrounded by all the people I loved. Sure, many were missing, those I had left behind on earth, but I knew they too would be joining us soon. And I didn't miss them. I did not miss anything from my life back on earth. Everything here was perfect, everything felt wonderful and amazing . . . I was made to be here. This was my home. And if given a choice to return to earth or stay here, well, that would be an easy decision—I would stay. "Well, I'll see you around," Sam said. "Eric and I have plans."

"Plans?" I asked, slightly confused.

"Yeah, you were correct, Anne. We do get along well. We're great friends."

"Technically brothers," Eric said, coming alongside Sam. "We're all family here." I smiled again. I couldn't help but smile. Everything was so perfect. "I'll catch up with you later, Anne," Eric said, giving me a quick hug.

I watched as he and Sam ran off. Once again, I was amazed at the speed at which we could run. In the blink of an eye, they were both out of sight.

"There's someone else who has been waiting to meet you," Miles said as he came to my side.

I smiled as he took my hand and led me away from the others. Walking over the bridge, we followed the gold road for a distance. As we walked, we passed several others, both human and angel, children and adults, though all of us adults were the same age . . . about thirty if I had to guess an age, yet in this body, I felt more amazing than I ever did at thirty on earth. Once again, I knew who each person was even though we had never met, and they knew me. No one here was in any rush like people were on earth, and everyone greeted one another with a smile. It couldn't be helped—we were all so filled with joy and peace.

"I didn't realize there would be so many children," I said. "Where do they all come from?"

"Most of them are from miscarriages and abortions," Miles replied. "But there are many who passed as babies or children just like our Jacob. They won't always be children. They grow, just as they do on earth, but eventually they stop aging, and they become like us."

"Who takes care of them?"

"Angels of course," he replied. "And you can visit the nursery anytime you wish. I know you love holding babies," he said, smiling.

I smiled back as we passed yet another young man. "Miles, that was—"

"Paul," he replied, finishing my thought.

"*The* Paul . . ." I whispered. "As in the apostle Paul?"

"Did you think they were made up?" he asked, chuckling.

"No, I just . . . well, I . . . I guess I never really imagined I would see them. Really see them."

"Just wait until you meet Jesus. Now that's a rush," he said, smiling. It was at that moment I realized I had not yet seen Jesus. I may not have seen him, but I could feel Him. His presence was all around. And His love . . . always present. "Now you will often see John the Baptist sitting right there under that tree," he said as we continued walking, pointing to a large willow tree that stood by the river's edge. "It's one of his favorite fishing spots."

"Have you meet them all?" I asked. "Everyone who was mentioned in the Bible?"

"No, not everyone. Not yet. Did you forget that I arrived shortly before you?"

"It may not have seemed long to you, Miles," I said. "But it was four days for me, four very long days!"

"Just think, Anne," he said. "It won't be long until our children join us here. And then our grandchildren and our great-grandchildren. Soon we will all be together once again, never to be separated for all eternity." I nodded, truly looking forward to that moment. "Speaking of children . . . come along."

We walked just a bit farther, and then Miles directed me off the path into a garden where we eventually came to an arbor. Flowers I had never seen before in colors I had never seen adorned the arbor. These flowers were singing too! Singing praises to God. How amazing this place was. His presence was everywhere. And I knew, really knew just how much he loved me. At the far end of the arbor was a bench with a young lady sitting on it. When she saw me, she stood, smiling. Immediately, I released Miles's hand and took off running toward her. I didn't stop until my arms were around her. "I love you, I love you, oh how I loved you," I said with tears pouring down my face.

"I know you love me, Mama. And I love you too," she replied. I held my daughter close for a long while. How I had longed for this day when I would meet the child I had lost. And now it was here. She was here, and I was holding her in my arms just as I had longed to do for years. I held her at arm's length. She was beautiful and perfect, and not just her looks. She was beautiful, but looks didn't matter . . . it was her spirit. Though we had never met until just now, I knew her. I knew everything about her—her personality, her likes, her talents, everything that God made her to be—and it was all good. She was everything I had imagined her to be and so much more. I recognized that even more than I was her mother, she was God's daughter. She belonged to him, just as all my children belonged to him. What an awesome God I served, that he shared his precious creations with me. I did not deserve this beautiful child or any of my others. It was only because of his great love for me that he blessed me with each of my precious children. As I looked at her, I suddenly realized she had no name.

"God wanted you to name me, Mama," she said as if she could read my mind. "There are many of us here in heaven waiting for our names."

"Many?" I asked, not quite understanding what she meant.

She nodded. "There are millions of us. Children who were lost like me," she explained. "Or aborted before they even had a chance at life. So what is it? What is my name?"

I already knew her name because I had picked it out long before I had even lost her. I had chosen Benjamin for a boy and "Abigail. Your name is Abigail Rose," I said.

She smiled then said her name in a hushed tone just barely above a whisper. Saying her name . . . cherishing it. Then suddenly I felt a presence, an overwhelming presence. I turned around to see a man standing behind me. A beautiful man who had light emanating from him. His eyes were full of love, and he exuded peace. When he held his hands out to me, I could see the scars from where he had been nailed to the cross. Immediately I dropped to my knees in front of my Lord and savior.

"Daughter," he said as he placed his hand on my shoulder. I looked up to see he was smiling at me. I felt absolutely no condemnation, no fear, and no shame. Nothing but love, pure, perfect love. Taking my hands in his, he brought me to my feet and embraced me. There are no words to explain how I felt. To be this close to Jesus, to actually touch him and feel his touch. What an amazing feeling it was to be in his physical presence, no longer separated by sin. I felt safe, secure, complete, whole, loved, cherished . . . I was in perfect peace. He held me at arm's length. "Welcome home, Anne," he said, smiling as he wiped my tears away. "Welcome home."

SCRIPTURE REFERENCES

All taken from the ESV Version of the Bible.

"All flesh is like grass and all its glory like the flower of grass. The grass withers, and the flower falls . . ." **1 Peter 1 2:24**

"Be strong and courageous. Do not fear or be in dread of them, for it is the LORD your God who goes with you. He will not leave you or forsake you." **Deuteronomy 31:6**

"For all have sinned and fall short of the glory of God, and are justified by his grace as a gift, through the redemption that is in Christ Jesus, whom God put forward as a propitiation by his blood, to be received by faith. This was to show God's righteousness, because in his divine forbearance he had passed over former sins. It was to show his righteousness at the present time, so that he might be just and the justifier of the one who had faith in Jesus." **Romans 2:23-26**

"As far as the east is from the west, so far does he remove our transgressions from us." **Psalm 103:12**

"Therefore, if anyone is in Christ, he is a new creation. The old has passed away; behold, the new has come." **2 Corinthians 5:17**

"For God so loved the world, that he gave his only Son, that whoever believes in him should not perish but have eternal life." **John 3:16**

"And Jesus said to him, 'Why do you call me good? No one is good except God alone.'" **Mark 10:18**

"Then I saw a new heaven and a new earth, for the first heaven and the first earth had passed away, and the sea was no more. And I saw the holy city, new Jerusalem, coming down out of heaven from God, prepared as a bride adorned for her husband. And I heard a loud voice from the throne saying, 'Behold the dwelling place of God is with man. He will dwell with them, and they will be his people, and God himself will be with them as their God. He will wipe every tear from their eyes, and death shall be no more, neither shall there be mourning, nor crying, nor pain anymore, for the former things have passed away.' And he who was seated on the throne said, 'Behold, I am making all things new.' Also, he said, 'Write this down, for these words are trustworthy and true.' And he said to me, 'It is done! I am the Alpha and Omega, the beginning and the end. To the thirsty I will give from the spring of the water of life without payment. The one who conquers will have this heritage, and I will be his God and he will be my son. But as for the cowardly, the faithless, the detestable, as for murderers, the sexually immoral, sorcerers, idolaters, and all liars, their portion will be in the lake that burns with fire and sulfur, which is the second death.' Then came one of the seven angels who had the seven bowls full of the seven last plagues and spoke to me, saying, 'Come, I will show you the Bride, the wife of the Lamb.' And he carried me away in the Spirit to a great, high mountain, and showed me the holy city Jerusalem coming down out of heaven from God, having the glory of God, its radiance like a most rare jewel, like jasper, clear as crystal. It had a great, high wall, with twelve gates, and at the gates twelve angels, and on the gates the names of the twelve tribes of the sons of Israel were inscribed on the east three gates, on the north three gates, on the south three gates, and on the west three gates. And the wall of the city had twelve foundations, and on them were the twelve names of the twelve apostles of the Lamb. And the one who spoke with me had a measuring rod of gold to measure the city and its gates and walls. The city lies foursquare, its length and the same as its width. And he measured the city with his rod, 12,000 stadia. Its length and width and height are equal. He also measured its wall, 144 cubits by human measurement, which is also an angel's measurement. The wall was built of jasper, while the city was pure gold, like clear glass. The foundations of the wall of the city were adorned with every kind of jewel. The first was jasper, the second sapphire, the third agate, the fourth emerald, the fifth onyx, the sixth carnelian, the seventh chrysolite, the eighth beryl, the ninth topaz, the tenth chrysoprase, the eleventh jacinth, the twelfth amethyst. And the twelve gates were twelve pearls, each of the gates made of a single pearl, and the street of the city was pure gold, like transparent glass. And I saw no temple in the city, for its temple is the Lord God the Almighty and the Lamb. And city has no need of sun or moon to shine on it, for the glory of God gives it light, and the lamp is the Lamb. By its light will the nations walk, and the kings of the earth will bring their glory to it, and its gates will never be shut by day—and there will be no night there. They will bring into it the glory and honor of the nations. But nothing unclean will ever enter it, nor anyone who does what is detestable or false, but only those who are written in the Lamb's book of life. 22 Then the angel showed me the river of the water of life, bright and crystal, flowing from the throne of God and of the Lamb through the middle of the street of the city; also, on either side of the river, the tree of life with its twelve kinds of fruit, yielding its fruit each month. The leaves of the tree were for the healing of the nations. No longer will there be anything accursed, but the throne of God and the Lamb will be in it, and his servants will worship him. They will see his face, and his name will be on their foreheads. And night will be no more. They will need no light of lamp or sun, for the Lord God will be their light, and they will reign forever and ever." **Revelation 21 & 22:1-5**

    * Side note: Though I know the heavenly city, new Jerusalem, that I have described in my book is not in theologically correct sequence, as it comes down to earth only after the thousand year reign, I chose to write in this manner because I needed to describe Heaven to the best of my ability, and without having been there myself, I went to the Word. As we know, to be absent from the body is to be present with the Lord. ("Yes, we are of good courage, and we would rather

be away from the body and at home with the Lord." 2 Corinthians 5:8). So until Jesus returns for his church . . . where do we go when we die? This is the great mystery. We know that upon His return, we receive our new bodies, and the Bible tells us that we are "asleep in Christ." ("But we do not want you to be uniformed, brothers, about who are sleep, that you may not grieve as others who have no hope. For since we believe that Jesus died and rose again, even so, through Jesus, God will bring with him those who have fallen asleep. For this we declare to you by the word from the Lord, that we who are alive, who are left until the coming of the Lord, will not precede those who have fallen asleep." 1 Thessalonians 4:13-15) Many people take this to mean that if we die before Christs return, we are "sleeping." And while that may be the case, the Bible does give us a picture of what happens to us after death (Luke 16:19-31) Yes, this was in the old testament, and these people were in Sheol, but since then, Jesus has died and risen. He went to Sheol, and he gathered all those in Adam's bosom, and he took them home with him. Their souls and spirits are alive today, and they are right now with Christ. If they were conscious, aware, and could speak while in Sheol, how much more alive are they today living with Christ! So with the information I have, and the research I have done, this is why I chose to end my story in this way. And who knows, maybe new Jerusalem has already been built, just waiting to come down and take its place on the new earth at the time God has ordained.

*As mentioned, C. S. Lewis – (1898-1963) Author of over thirty books, including the Chronicles of Narnia Series.

Made in the USA
Columbia, SC
02 May 2018